MW01133644

# For the Love
# of a Woman

**A Balum Series Western**

**no.4**

**A novel by**

Orrin Russell

Cover design and illustration by
Mike Pritchett

# 1

In the first hour after he ate them, Balum felt nothing.

He had left Frederick Nelson slumped belly over the saddle, tied hand-to-foot and swearing, and walked into the featureless swath of land stretching out to the rim of the earth where he sat with his back rested against a bur oak. He had opened the small leather pouch, eaten its contents, and sat watching the sun dip below the farthest reaches of the land, all the while wondering if there had been some misunderstanding.

The Shoshone who had presented him with the gift spoke no English, and neither did Balum speak the Indian's tongue. The medicine man had made fantastic gestures with his hands, bringing them against his temples and expanding them outwards as if to tell Balum what was in the pouch would expand the very consciousness of his mind.

Doubtful, thought Balum. But he was in no hurry, and Nelson's constant complaining was wearing thin. The Shoshone, robed in a buffalo skin tunic with a face as solemn and deep as though carved from sandstone, was one of a group of starving Indians who had clamored along behind the wagons making up Frederick Nelson's Oregon Expedition. It was Balum's kindness that had helped them survive. Whatever the nature of the gift, it was meant in good faith.

With that thought in mind, he had dumped the contents of the leather satchel into his mouth and chewed what tasted like dirt mixed with the sweepings of a cattle yard, and waited. The sun finished its decent and night took up its shift over the earth.

Time passed. Stars glimmered overhead. Balum stood, then sat back down. A wave whipped suddenly over the plains. The ground buckled and the heavens drew closer, shimmering like a lake under moonlight, bobbing gently on currents of starlit galaxies. The corners of the earth curled up and cupped him in its breast. He stood again, stumbled, then laughed. In circles he turned, a lone madman spinning on the darkened Wyoming plains, cackling and screaming, and finally falling to the ground and wallowing in crazed convulsions as he spun in circles and rolled from back to belly. The concept of time took leave. He walked, crawled, sat in a daze of existential laughter, thoroughly enjoying the levity of a weightless mind, until suddenly, like an ax falling over an oak log, it shifted. Memories swept over him; the darkest and most garish, locked away in the hollows of his mind for too long. Memories of *La Cárcel de Belén* erupted. Dark cells, wet stone, cries of anguish. An odor of mold and mildew. The stench of unwashed prisoners cramped in cages and kept from sunlight.

He reeled, hands clutching his head, and fought for

happier memories.

Into reminiscences of women he fled. He fought to remember their names, their faces, the touch of their fingertips upon him and the sweet caresses dolled out in the throes of passion. He remembered Charlise and Cynthia, Consuelo, Suzanne Darrow. Deborah DeLace's moans of pleasure, and the way Leigha had held him in the night.

The rush of names sped through him, the faces, the bodies, breasts and thighs and lips all converging together, and though it took him from the pain brought by memories of a Mexican jail, it brought with with it a new anguish. The lengthy list of conquests was not recollected with a sense of pride or self-aggrandizement. As the faces drifted through his mushroom-riddled mind, he felt the sorrow and the loneliness and the vacuous pit of emptiness that was his inner self.

He had had women. By the dozen. Yet he yearned for one and one only; a companion, a friend, a lover who understood him and he her. Someone to grow old with, to walk hand in hand through fields of wildflowers; two souls blended into one.

Tears ran down the lines of his face. A face beaten and scarred by the harshness of life, tanned by the sun and the wind, struck by fists, chapped and cut and healed over countless times. He dried them absentmindedly, taking in large breaths that came stuttering out in desperate exhales, as if each one were an admission of guilt.

Under a ceiling of starry skies he stretched his body over the grass and finally, as the effects of the Shoshone's medicine wore off, as the earth released him from its breast, as the shimmering rocks came back into resoluteness, he was granted sleep.

Throughout the night he dreamt of Angelique.

In the morning he woke and walked toward the rising sun. An hour's march over the grasslands brought him to the horses standing in the shade of a cottonwood stand. Frederick Nelson's body rested motionless, draped as it was over the saddle. Balum's roan gave a snort when it caught wind of him and turned. The movement prodded Nelson from his slumber.

'Balum, is that you?' his voice croaked like a dying bullfrog.

'It's me,' said Balum when he reached the roan.

'Goddamn you, Balum. Where have you been? This isn't any way to treat a man. Look at me!' he barked. His face was splotched with red and white patterns laced like spider webbing over the skin. His hair stuck to his forehead, matted in sweat and blown awry by the wind. Snot dripped down his nose. Mucus formed in his throat and was hacked out in thick strands as he cursed his captor.

'Untie me, would you?' he begged. 'I've got saddle sores on my ribs for the love of God.'

'Sounds miserable.'

'What kind of a lawman are you anyway?'

'Not much of one,' said Balum, and pulled the rope

end from the knot at Nelson's wrists.

The big man fell from the horse and collapsed into a pile on the ground. He rolled to his side and spat, rubbing his blood-filled head and taking in great gulps of air.

Balum paid him no mind. He untied a pan from the saddlebags and filled a kettle with water from a canteen. In short time he had a small fire burning. The smoke drifted and dispersed through the cottonwoods above. He fried salt pork in the pan and made coffee which he drank before giving it the chance to cool completely.

From the ground Frederick Nelson watched Balum click his singed tongue.

'You plan on giving me some of that food?' he asked.

'You ate yesterday.'

'Give me some water.'

'Maybe later.'

'Goddamn it, Balum. I'm going to tell Pete Cafferty how I've been treated. There's laws, you know.'

Balum glanced sideways at the man on the ground, uninterested.

'It's only a week to Denver,' said Nelson. 'You can starve me out, but I'll last.'

'You're right, it's a week to Denver,' Balum nodded. 'Not counting the detour.'

'What in the hell detour are you talking about?'

'Figured we'd swing through Cheyenne first. I've got some things to attend to. Now let's get you back in that saddle.'

It took a couple boot kicks to Nelson's backside, but

Balum got the man moving and once again thrown belly-first over the saddle, hands tied to feet and the blood rushing back into his face.

They rode out over the junegrass with the sun watching them from above. Nelson eventually quit his griping, not from lack of outrage, but from lack of strength. Balum wouldn't have paid him any mind anyway. His thoughts leaned back to the visions of the night before. For a man who enjoyed time to ponder over his thoughts, Balum had days and nights in their entirety. The more he sat with his feelings, the more solidified they became. He rode with his prisoner over long stretches of nothingness, through fields of tall grass and dotted stands of trees, through streams and the occasional river, stopping only to drink from the canteen and lay out at night under the warmth of a blanket.

By the time they reached Charles and Will's ranch on the outskirts of Cheyenne, Balum's mind had come into agreement with his heart. A bit of joy rose up in him on the thought of sharing his decision with his old partner.

He pulled up on a small rise a half mile out from the ranch and smiled softly at the progress made over the short time since he had last seen his friends. The house was finished, as was the bunkhouse and stable in back. A corral had been built and in it grazed nearly two dozen well-built horses. The well had a cover built over it, and flowers of all things had been planted around the front door of the house. Scattered farther to the north he could see cattle grazing in great numbers on the free range. Smelted iron had been bent into the letters CW and hung between two poles on either side of the makeshift road leading into the compound. Beneath these letters Balum paused to look at the ironwork. Charles and Will. The CW Ranch.

Out from the shadows of the stable doors, Charles' figure emerged. The man put a hand to his eye, squinted, then leaned back with his hands on his hips when he recognized Balum's roan. Had the distance been any shorter, Balum would have seen the smile stretch across the man's face.

No words were spoken until after Balum had swung down from the saddle and the two had hugged, gripped each other by the shoulders and had a laugh at the mere delight of the unexpected visit.

A look was thrown toward Nelson strung over the saddle.

'That's one stinking son of a bitch you've got thrown over that saddle, Balum. I take it that's Nelson? Why's he stink so bad?'

'That's him. It's slipped my mind a couple times to untie him. He's taken to relieving himself in the saddle.'

'Christ Almighty,' Charles wrinkled his nose and shook his head. 'I'm guessing he deserves it. Come on inside. Let me get you a plate of grub and you'll tell me all about it.'

They sat at a table set for two, prepared by a middle aged Mexican woman in a gingham apron. She wore her hair up in a bun and her eyes lingered on Charles when she set the plate before him.

'Start where you left off,' said Charles, forking huevos

con machaca into his mouth.

Balum thought for a moment on where to pick up the story. Not all that long ago, U.S. Marshal Pete Cafferty had assigned him the task of riding along with a wagon train full of Easterners clear to Oregon. The man leading the expedition was the very man cursing out in the sun over the back of a horse. Cafferty had known something wasn't right; Nelson having a dodgy reputation, and outfitted with a band of murderers for a crew. In the end, Balum and Joe had loaded a wagon, paid their dues, and set out. They had stopped in at Charles' ranch on the way west, told Charles and Will of their situation, and ridden on into the unknown.

'I take it you didn't make it to Oregon,' Charles prompted him.

'Not me. Joe took over as wagonmaster. They'll make it.'

'So what happened?'

'Nelson had a gatling gun stowed in his wagon. They veered off trail, got folks up in a chain of mountain valleys that led into a box canyon. Joe and I saw it, saw where he'd taken the last group of settlers and massacred them. He aimed to do the same this time,' Balum's eyes clouded over at the memory. 'That type of gun can cut down a herd of people in the space of a minute. All hell broke loose. Several folks died, a lot more maimed and injured. Me and Joe, we picked off his crew, ended up taking Nelson alive. I'd just as soon of shot him and left him for the wolves, but Atkisson, the man left in charge, he insisted I take him back to Denver for a trial.'

'They'll give him a trial and a hanging,' said Charles. 'And you? What'll you do now? You aim to keep on as Deputy Marshal?'

'No I do not,' Balum said emphatically. 'I've been at it for six months, and that's five months and three weeks more than I ever planned on. We made plenty of money off that drive, Charles. First time I've had any money in my life. Near ten thousand dollars sitting for me at the Denver Commercial Bank, and it's calling me.'

'Enough to keep you up to your neck in women.'

Balum shook his head. 'No more chasing women for me.'

'You ain't serious.'

'I am. I aim to settle down.'

'And just how did this all come about?' asked Charles.

Between mouthfuls of food, Balum told Charles the story.

'You mean to say,' said Charles, 'that you ate a bunch of mushrooms an Indian gave you, the world turned inside out, and you come out of it set on finding a gal and marrying her?'

'That about sums it up.'

Charles laughed out loud. 'Well first off, anybody with their head tapped on solid knows not to go eating nothing no Shoshone medicine man gives you.'

'I'm glad I did.'

'You want to end up like Will?'

'What's Will up to?'

'Getting married.'

'Married?'

'Found himself a nice young lady. Tessa. He's plum in love, can't concentrate long enough to ride a horse without falling off. They'll be hitched within the month.'

Balum had cleaned his plate. He set his fork down. 'That's what I want.'

'Falling off horses and writing love letters?'

'Don't act like you don't want it too, Charles. You've had one eye on that señora this whole time. And she's looked your way plenty of times. What's the story there?'

Charles blushed. It turned his face red, and he looked at his plate. 'Didn't know it was so obvious,' he muttered.

'Like a five legged bull.'

'Alright, you got me. Her name's Juanita. I met her at the rodeo over summer. She said she could cook, so… Anyway, that's that.'

'That's good.'

Charles frowned across the table at his old partner. Balum could see the man's mind turning over. After a while a glimmer struck in his eye.

'I know why you're here,' Charles said. He spread his hands over the table and drummed his fingers.

'Just came to say hello is all.'

Charles rocked his head back and forth. 'No, no. That ain't it. You come for Angelique.'

Balum didn't respond.

'Ha!' clapped Charles. 'And there's nothing wrong with that. I was surprised when you left for Denver. The way you two look at each other, why anyone can see it.'

'It's complicated.'

'Everything's complicated.'

'She says we're too wild, the one for the other.'

'Bullshit.'

'Maybe.'

'What do you plan on doing then?'

'Ride over. Let her know how I feel.'

'With that stinking son of a bitch riding along with?'

'Nothing I can do about that.'

Charles pushed his chair back and stood. 'You're making a good decision. Guess that wasn't a bad idea eating those mushrooms. Tell her how you feel, what you want, then drop that bum off in Denver so they can hang him, and come back and settle down. We'll be neighbors'

'That easy.'

'That easy.'

'You tell Will I send him my regards,' said Balum on his way out. 'I'll be expecting an invitation to the wedding.'

# 2

Cheyenne rose up out of the earth larger than Balum remembered. His last visit had been but one drunken night of debauchery of which he remembered little apart from being beaten near to death by the Farro brothers. Still, it had only been a matter of a few months since he had first ridden in with Charles and the boys and called Cheyenne a temporary home. In that short time, streets had been laid out, not in any orderly fashion, but following the same unorganized sprawl of before, only more numerous. Buildings had been slapped together, most of them ramshackle affairs, others built solid and supporting two stories.

From a mile out he could see the railway on the far eastern edge of the city. The station platform had doubled in size and a ticket booth had been built. It was not only cattle shipped from the rail yards anymore, but people, merchandise and money.

The streets were busy. He rode through them, the roan seeming to size up the town with the same measured eye as its rider. Frederick Nelson, hung across the saddle like a bag of cornmeal, drew attention. People stared. When they realized who they were looking at, they shouted.

'Hey! It's Balum!' yelled a drunk from the boardwalk.

Balum smiled. He felt like a hero in this town. Hell, he thought. He *was* a hero. Ned Witney had pushed this town around and had folks pinned under his thumb until Balum and Charles had their cattle stolen. In a flurry of blood and bullets they had reclaimed what had been stolen from them and freed the town from oppression. It was not something to be forgotten.

'Who's the prisoner, Balum?' asked the townsfolk and children as they encircled the riders. 'Is he gonna get the Ned Witney treatment?'

'I'm taking this man to Denver. There'll be a hanging, you can count on it.'

The drunk who had first shouted did so again. 'You want a drink and it's on me.'

'Much obliged,' said Balum. He'd reached a mercantile shop a few blocks from Angelique's place, and swung down from the roan. The townsfolk were good people, but not without prying eyes. 'If you folks would like to do me a favor, keep an eye on this stinking mess right here. He's tied up tighter than a suckling pig, but it doesn't hurt to be careful. I'll be back shortly.'

He left the two horses at the posts outside the mercantile and snuck away from the crowd and down the back alleys. Down narrow streets, dust covered and walled by wood slatted store fronts. Past a dog with a sore eye, the puss-filled orb following him in disinterest.

It was the back door he arrived at. He knocked and

waited, memories resurging of days gone by when he'd let himself in with the key Angelique had given him. After a moment the door swung open and, like deja vu, Else's figure appeared. She wore a thin nightgown, though it was the middle of the day, and a corset that pushed her breasts up and together under her neck.

He smiled and removed his hat.

'Balum,' she said softly, and opened the door wide. He stepped through it and gave her a hug, aware of the feel of her body against his. When he drew back from her she looked quizzically at him and asked, 'No kisses or squeezes?'

He laughed. 'I'm a well-behaved man now.'

She shook her head with a smirk, disbelieving.

'I've come to pay a visit to Angelique. Is she around?'

'She left an hour ago.'

'I can wait.'

'Come with me,' she said. She took his hand and led him through the back hallway, through the curtain and into the main barroom where tables and sofas sat underneath dim lighting. Customers were few in the mid afternoon. The girls lounged on the furniture, gossiped amongst themselves, and smiled at Balum when he took a seat at a table.

Helene was standing at the bar running a wet rag over the surface. When she saw Balum she waved at him bashfully. A word passed between the two girls in Danish and they left together back through the curtain. Balum fidgeted with his hat at the table. He wished he had a plug

16

of tobacco in his cheek. Before long a thin girl with blond hair asked him if he'd like a drink. He hesitated, nodded his head. She returned a minute later from the bar with a shot of brandy and sat with him.

'I've never see you here before,' she said. Her breath smelled of perfume and cigarettes.

'I'm an old friend of Angelique. I came to say hello.'

'She stepped out a while ago. I think she went to look at a piece of land to the north. She's been talking about buying a ranch house for some time.'

'When will she be back?'

'Oh, not for a long time I expect. However fast her horse decides to take her.'

Balum sipped at the brandy.

The girl leaned in. She rested a hand on Balum's thigh and brought her cheek alongside his. 'I can help you pass the time if you'd like,' she whispered.

He felt a stirring within him. Like a bull released into the breeding pen, riled and ornery after the trek back with Nelson. But for as hot as his blood ran, the weight of his heart as it ached for Angelique outdistanced the urges generated by the barely dressed women lounging about. He threw back the last of the brandy and rose from the table.

'I'll be back in a minute,' he said, and left through the front door while the blond sat alone with the empty glass.

In the street again he breathed deeply and let his head come back to rest on his shoulders. He couldn't sit much longer in that room. Temptation was a beast against which he held few weapons.

Men and women sweeping their porches and unhitching their horses from street posts nodded to him as he made his way back to Nelson. Before he reached him he stepped into a corner shop selling dry goods and feed, and purchased a pouch of chewing tobacco. Under the shade of the boardwalk awning he tucked a plug into his cheek and closed his eyes. The lightness hit him and he took another deep breath, then continued up the street.

When he turned the corner and came upon the hitching post where he had left Nelson and his roan, he stopped with a jerk, squinted, and spat into the dust.

Children surrounded the man tied over the horse. They carried all sorts of rotten produce no doubt stolen from a pig pen. In their hands they carried squishy tomatoes, putrid squash, rotten cucumbers, mushy and moldy and all of it stinking. As Balum watched, a boy cocked his arm back and pitched a head of lettuce at Nelson's skull. It exploded when it landed, the leaves flying in every direction. The adults watching the scene only laughed and egged the children on.

Balum waded through the youngsters and bent down eye level to Nelson.

'Seems they've taken a liking to you,' he said.

Nelson shook his head, bits of tomato juice clinging to his ears. 'If I get the chance I'll kill you, Balum.'

'I'm sure you would.'

Balum stood and surveyed the onlookers. He knew he should admonish them, tell them to leave the prisoner be, to behave. But the screams of the dying still rang in his ears from the valley chain, and he told the children instead to enjoy themselves and practice their aim.

At the Rosemonte Hotel he asked for a paper and pen, and sat at a table in the dining area. The steel nib scratched the stationary in the outlines of his rough penmanship. He wondered at the spelling of the words and struggled to put his thoughts on paper. When he was finished he folded the letter in half, tucked it into an envelope, then returned the pen to the clerk and walked back to Angelique's place.

'You're sure Angelique will be back tonight?' he asked the blond when she answered the door.

'I'm positive.'

'See that she gets this,' he handed her the letter. 'It's important.'

'I promise I will. Don't you worry. Now are you sure you don't want to come in for another drink? Or maybe upstairs? I could help you take your mind off things.' She took a step back so his eyes could slide down her body.

'I don't doubt that you could,' he said. 'But I'll be going. Make sure Angelique gets that letter.'

He left with the same rushing sensation as he had before. The smell of the place, the perfume, the oils, the flesh of the women. It filled his head with a blinding fervor that weakened his knees and clouded his vision.

Outside the mercantile shop he shooed away the children and unlooped the reins from the posts. His boot found the stirrup, he threw a leg over the saddle, then turned and rode with Nelson's horse trailing the roan, a last few tomatoes flying in wide arcs and landing with splats around them.

They wove their way through crooked streets and jagged intersections. Carts and wagons and pedestrians converged in an unorganized mess of rising dust and yells and the clink and clatter of metal and the creaks of wood. Balum kept the roan's nose pointed eastward through it all, until the streets petered out into random paths and the cattle yards surrounding the railway came into view.

The station was empty, as were the tracks. He left Nelson tied where he was, despite his pleas to be released, and climbed the steps to the newly built platform. He tucked a fresh plug of tobacco into his cheek and set his hands in his pockets along side the Colt Dragoon at his hip. The sun beat down, heating the wood boards beneath him, burning the dust and the grass and everything it touched. After a while he walked to the shade and watched the sun slip through the low hanging clouds and settle on the horizon. He thought of Angelique. Again, as during his vision, the memories of past lovers drifted through his mind. He felt nothing. A wisp of nostalgia maybe, nothing more. His feelings had moved on. Desires, wants, the yearning within him that was the source of striving, the momentum behind his actions, it had all shifted. He wanted what Charles and Will had.

When the last rays of the sun were cut off by the earth's edge, Nelson called out from the horse. He begged to be untied. He needed to relieve himself, it hurt to breathe. The words flew past Balum like wind over a stone.

Darkness crept over them. Still they waited. Crickets began their chirping and the first flickerings of lightning bugs began to turn on and off. Somewhere a bullfrog sang.

'Balum!' shouted Nelson. 'What the hell are we doing out here? What are we waiting on?'

Balum looked into the darkness toward town.

'Whoever you're waiting on isn't coming, Balum. When are you gonna figure that out?'

'Shut up,' he said quietly.

'Shutting me up won't change things. Nobody's coming. It's getting cold.'

An hour passed, then another. The constellations worked themselves over the heavens, rising up from where the sun would later emerge and traveling the same path as the world twisted below them.

He felt a tightness in his throat. A chill came over him and he wrapped his hands over his arms and strained to see through the darkness.

She did not come.

Through the night he waited, until the cold prodded him to take to the saddle again. Back to town they rode, Nelson complaining all the while, whimpering nearly. At the livery they stopped. Her horse would either be there or not.

The liveryman was gone. The swinging door had been locked from the inside. Balum walked the perimeter, looking for a way in. He edged up on his toes to see through the slim windows but could see nothing in the blackness.

Confusion set over him. Had she understood the letter? Had she read it and crumpled it and tossed it aside? Did she care for him? A mix of emotions careened through his mind which he found himself wholly unable to assess in that brief section of night. His better judgement mixed with the thoughts of a fool, and the discernment between the two refused to reveal itself.

Down the back alleys he rode, past the lazy dog with the dripping eye. He circled round to the front and tied the two horses loosely to a rail. At the door he paused, then cracked it. Music hit him. Music and lights and the smell of women. He had nearly swung the door wide open to enter when he saw her there beside the bar, speaking to a well-dressed man with a top hat and fine coat. Her hair was thick and smooth and it fell in locks over a body accentuated by a sheer dress hugging the curves as if struggling fruitlessly to restrain the body underneath.

He pulled the door closed suddenly and spun around. The horses stamped when he ripped their reins from the rail. He swung into the saddle and pulled Nelson's horse behind.

'Plenty of whorehouses in Denver, Balum, if that's what you're after,' said Nelson behind him. 'Let's get moving.'

# 3

Under moonlight, accompanied by the howl of wolves and the yipping of coyotes, the two mens' horses plodded southward. The shimmer of the crescent light played on the surface of the streams they crossed, breaking in ripples as hooves broke the stillness and splashed forward. A cold wind bit at them. Nelson's complaining went unanswered. He yelled and barked and cursed his captor until his strength left him and he fell asleep over the rocking of the horse beneath.

When fatigue outweighed his sorrow, Balum staked the horses out and dumped Nelson out of the saddle and tied him again. They slept without fire on the leeward side of a hill and rose in the morning as the sun was just saluting the earth.

All day they rode. There was no rush in Balum's pace; he rode like a somnambulist, resolute in the saddle and deaf to the cries of Frederick Nelson. He could have pushed the pace to arrive after nightfall in Denver, but he saw no reason. He saw little reason for much at all, such was his despondency. The land about him appeared bleak and featureless, the songs of the birds little more than an annoyance similar to the whining of the man behind him. There was no hunger in him. He ate nothing throughout the day and stopped again at night and built a fire only to warm himself. He sipped water from a canteen and fell into a dreamless sleep.

The morning sun woke him. He rose, pissed, rubbed his eyes. Nelson let himself be thrown atop the saddle without a fuss; he knew Denver was close. Balum tucked a plug of tobacco into his cheek, mounted the roan, and the sounds of creaking saddle leather and the snorting of horses resumed.

They arrived mid-afternoon. The difference in the look and feel of Denver from Cheyenne struck him. Denver had always been bigger, livelier, somehow cleaner looking. Modern-- that was the word that came to him. The city housed all the characters seen throughout the West; the cowpokes and the ranchers, the gamblers, storekeepers, loggers, farmers, bankers and businessmen. There were whores; more than one could count. There were others though, brought in from the East in fancy clothes and fine carriages. They walked the streets with their heads up, backs straight. As though they had come to conquer the land, to have the cities rise up under their thumbs.

They stared at him as he rode in with his captive tied like a hog, the man's face red and swollen with blood. He was covered in dust and dirt, soiled, stinking, and too weak to curse. Clear to the Denver jail the townsfolk followed them, where they stood in the street with mouths agape as

Balum untied Frederick Nelson and dumped him to the ground. Flies darted at the commotion then settled back to Nelson's body. The townsfolk murmured and gossiped, their voices rising until from inside the jail office Pete Cafferty came through the door to see what all the fuss was about.

He nearly spilled his coffee when he saw Balum dragging Frederick Nelson through the dust.

'Balum!' he shouted, and set down the mug and grabbed Nelson. The two men hauled the convict through the jail door and into the office.

Inside were two desks. At one sat Ross Buckling, the town sheriff who, though good at his job, did not insert himself in affairs that did not concern him. And this, most certainly, did not concern him.

From the other rose a young man with a starched collar and a face of shocked concern. His nose was thin and he had a weak jaw, and he wore the badge of U.S. Marshall, just like the one pinned on Pete Cafferty's breast pocket.

'What's all this?' the young man said, coming round the desk with his mouth hanging open and his brow furrowed together.

'Johnny, this here is Balum. The man I told you you'd be seeing sooner or later,' said Cafferty. 'Later is what I always figured. And this stinking mess is Frederick Nelson, the other one I told you about. Balum, Johnny Freed. U.S. Marshal, soon to take over the region.'

Johnny Freed leaned in with his hand outstretched, his

eyes still suspicious, as if he hadn't quite figured out what all was going on yet. Balum took the kid's cold hand in his, gave it a pump, and dropped it.

'Johnny,' said Cafferty, 'why don't you help Ross get this man into a cell.'

'Why, we can't just throw him in a cell,' stuttered Johnny. 'This man needs medical attention. Anyone can see that.'

'Just get him in a cell,' said Cafferty. Ross Buckling was already bending down to grab one of Nelson's arms. 'Go on, Johnny. Grab that other arm. Get him out of here.'

The two men each hooked a hand through Nelson's armpits and carried him, feet dragging, across the office and down the cell corridor to where four rooms each with a set of iron bars across them sat nearly empty.

Alone in the office with Cafferty, Balum raised his eyebrows.

Cafferty looked down and shook his head. 'He came out of West Point. Came from a good family. Some strings were pulled, I don't know. That's politics. All I know is I've had more on my plate than I've had in a long time, and I'm ready to get out. Some fools have robbed the train going into Cheyenne twice now. They've missed the cattle payload each time, which is surely what they're after, but they robbed all the passengers and gave everyone around the area a fright. Anyway, it doesn't concern me much longer. I'm leaving tomorrow for the Southwest. My relocation has gone through and I'm handing these problems over to Freed.'

26

'It doesn't concern me much either,' said Balum. From his pocket he pulled out the Deputy Marshal badge. He set it in Cafferty's hand. 'U.S. Deputy Marshal no more. I'm a free man now.'

'I appreciate you sticking with it as long as you did. Even if it was only a few months. So tell me. What happened out there?'

'It was like you said. Me and Joe found where he'd massacred that last bunch. This time he had a gatling gun in his wagon. He turned the group off track and into a mountain chain headed straight for a box canyon. He cut loose on them with the gun, killed several, injured several more.'

'And the Farro brothers?'

'Dead. I shot Gus myself. Saul was shot, thrown down a cliff. The other two he had with him were killed as well.'

Cafferty shook his head. 'Sounds like there was a massacre alright, just not the one he saw coming.'

'Let me get something for you,' Balum said, and turned back through the door to the street outside. From the saddlebags he drew out three sheets of paper folded over and covered in a thin film of dust. He swatted them against the roan's flank, shook them out, then returned to the office.

Inside, Johnny Freed had returned to the office. He leaned into Cafferty, his face intense and his voice urgent. When Balum's footsteps sounded on the wood floor he cut his speech off suddenly as though he had been caught at something.

Balum paid him no mind. He crossed the floor and extended the papers to Cafferty.

'What are these?' asked the Marshal.

'Signed affidavits,' said Balum. 'One from Atkisson, another from Jeb Darrow, and the third from Joe.'

'Smart thinking, Balum. It's yours that will hold up most in court though.'

'I can give a deposition tomorrow. As for now, I'm tired, hungry, and to tell you the truth, not in a mood for conversation. What I need now is a shot of whiskey, a bath and a bed.' He glanced at Ross and Johnny. 'You fellas enjoy the day. I'll stop in tomorrow. Pete, I'll be seeing you.'

He turned and left, and when nearly to the roan he heard Cafferty calling behind him from the boardwalk.

'I leave at first light tomorrow, Balum. I doubt I'll be seeing you.'

Balum turned and took a look at the Marshal. 'Joe told me what your end of the deal was.'

'And I aim to keep it.'

'I know you do.'

'That new Marshal, Johnny,' said Cafferty. 'He's riled up. Seems he got all his ideas of justice out of a book somewhere. Nelson's in pretty rough shape. Johnny's going on about due process and I don't know what else. Don't let him get to you. He's from back East. He's still learning. Keep that in mind when you stop in tomorrow.'

'I'll do that.'

'And Balum,' the Marshal let the shadow of a grin come over his face. 'Stay out of trouble for me.'

They shook hands, and Balum rode from the jail, Cafferty smiling to himself and watching the man disappear into the Denver chaos.

The room was nice. More than nice. The Berlamont was arguably one of the finest hotels in Denver, and Balum's room was one of the finest within that fine hotel. It came with a balcony, the sheets were fresh, a desk and chair sat in a corner, and a vase of flowers decorated the windowsill.

So this is high living, thought Balum. He kicked his boots off and tossed his hat over the desk. A bath would do him wonders but he had no energy to search it out. Instead he flopped across the bed and closed his eyes.

Outside, birds sang. He rolled over and held himself still and waited for sleep. Sunlight bathed the room. After a half hour of dullness he rose and closed the window curtains. Back on the mattress he fought to still his mind, to quiet his thoughts and sleep, but it would not come.

Another hour passed and he rose and shoved his feet into his boots. He grabbed his hat from the desk and left the room, crossed through the lobby and emerged into the street as sundown was just settling over the city.

The respectable businesses had closed their doors. Saloons and gambling houses began to swell with patrons. Women emerged on brothel balconies and flirted with the men on the streets below. Schoolmarms and storekeepers were replaced by another sort of character altogether; the young, the downtrodden, the reckless. Balum picked his way through them down the boulevards and side streets until he came to a thatched cabin at the end of a meandering street and slapped his palm to the door. A rustling could be heard behind it and in short order it swung open.

Chester's face reacted belatedly as the recognition of his visitor became clear. The eyes went from blankness to a glint of rambunctiousness and his teeth showed in a smile.

'Balum! Just what these old eyes needed to see. Get in here,' he motioned inside.

'You got whiskey in there?'

'So it's gonna be that kind of a night, eh? No, no whiskey. Sorry to disappoint.'

'Let's go then.'

'To the Baltimore?'

'Anywhere but the Baltimore.'

'Wherever you want, friend.'

They came out of the back alleys and stopped in a Mexican cantina on the edge of town away from the madness of the saloon district. The vaqueros sitting around short tables in leather chaps and stained sombreros watched the gringos curiously from the dark. The two took seats and watched the barman approach them. He wore a greasy apron and had a thick mustache that drooped over his upper lip.

'*Que les doy?*' he asked them.

'*Mezcal,*' said Balum.

30

'*Botella entera?*'

'*Dos vasos nomás.*'

The barman left them and returned a minute later with two glasses of mezcal.

'Glad you speak the lingo, Balum,' said Chester. 'I was to come in here myself and they'd throw me out.'

'I doubt it. They're good people.'

'So when did you get in?'

'This afternoon.'

'Alright,' Chester sipped the mezcal and puckered his face. 'Tell me the story.'

He told it, everything from the departure from Denver to the arrest of Frederick Nelson. Chester sipped mezcal and listened, saying nothing, only nodding his head as the weight of the events made their mark.

'And now you're here,' said Chester when it was finished.

'Now I'm here.'

'What next? You're done playing Deputy Marshal. You've got money. The world is yours.'

'I've been giving it some thought. Almost inclined to just saddle up and ride. See where the next bend in the trail takes me.'

Chester shook his head. 'Balum, you ain't no spring buck anymore. You ain't old like me, but you will be before you know it. Why don't you take up with Charles over there by Cheyenne? Settle down. Start ranching. Drifting ain't gonna get you nowhere.'

Balum looked down and shook his head.

'Go ahead, Balum. Tell me what's eating you.'

The mezcal had begun to loosen Balum's mind. As if grease had been poured into a seized up gear, his thoughts flowed out, slowly at first and accelerating as they came. He gave Chester the story of the mushrooms, his visions, his feelings, and finally of the letter and the long wait for Angelique at the train station in the cool of the evening.

When it was done, Chester turned to the barman and held up two fingers for two more mezcals.

'That gal's been on your mind since you first laid eyes on her.'

'She has.'

'You know what'll cure you? A trip to the Baltimore Club. Those girls can take a man's mind off of anything that worries him.'

'It's not what I want anymore, Chester.'

'You want Angelique.'

'I do. But she doesn't want me. That's clear enough. I want a woman I can grow old with. Charles is about to have it. Will is getting married. Jumping from woman to woman doesn't lead a man to satisfaction.'

'You sound like a man wise beyond your years. Finally growing up.'

'Maybe so.'

'So that's it? You're just gonna ride?'

'I've got to get away from here. It's too close to Angelique. Maybe I'll see what California is like. That Daniel Randolph claims it's good.'

'I'll be sorry to see you go, my friend,' said Chester.

'But if that's the way of it…'

They finished the mezcals and Balum rose and paid the tab at the bar. They left the cantina and parted ways in the dark and featureless street. Alone again, Balum skirted around the saloon district and reached the Berlamont Hotel by the backstreets. He entered the room and sat on the edge of the bed feeling lost and lonely, searching for hope in the dreams of the unknown. Finally, he undressed and stretched out across the bed.

His mind was settled. He would give his deposition in the morning and ride out.

# 4

The Berlamont Hotel provided a washroom on the lower level. The grime that filled the washtub when he was finished gave evidence to the belatedness of his bath. He could nearly refill it and go through the motions again, he thought, as he dried himself and looked into the mirror. His beard had grown well past the point of stubble and his hair hung in an overgrown matt of dark waves. A task too large for his blunted razor, he told himself. He'd take a trip to the barber. And why not? He still hadn't gotten used to the idea of a bank account full of money. He'd leave his present look of an unwashed barbarian in Denver.

With a bellyful of eggs he made his way to the jail. Ross Buckling sat at his desk with a tattered newspaper several weeks old held out from his face.

'Morning, Balum.'

'Ross,' Balum nodded. 'That kid Marshal around?'

The sheriff laughed. 'He's young, ain't he? Full of gumption. No, he's up at the courthouse jabbering at the judge. He's got his knickers all bunched up about Nelson. He was in quite a state the way you brought him in.'

'He was alive. More than can be said about the folks

34

laying dead up on the Oregon Trail.'

'That's true. Have yourself a seat. He'll be along.'

Balum took his hat off and eased himself into the empty chair behind the other desk. No sooner had he sat when the door swung open and Johnny Freed stepped through. The young Marshal straightened up and looked about as if evaluating the office's state of order, then turned to Balum.

'Mr. Balum. Good morning. I'll kindly take my desk back.'

Balum rose and held his hand out palm up to the chair, ceding the spot to the young man.

'Let's get this over with,' said Balum, and leaned up against the wall with his hands in his trouser pockets as the Marshal took his seat.

Johnny Freed took down the deposition. He asked a series of questions most of which Balum considered pointless, the words he used chosen from a lawbook and carefully laid out to display his authority on legal knowledge. Ross Buckling sat with the newspaper out in front of him, not reading a word of it. When the facts had been laid out and the questions answered, Freed turned the legal paper around on his desk and had Balum put his signature to it.

'Alright,' Balum tossed the pen back on the desk and stood up. 'We all through here?'

'No, Mr. Balum, we are not,' replied the young Marshal. 'There's an issue I must speak to you about, and it concerns the treatment of Mr. Nelson.'

Balum turned back from the door. 'Treatment?'

'That man was half starved when you brought him in. Did it not occur to you to feed him while you had him tied up all that while?'

'I can't say as though it did.'

'Neither apparently did it occur to you to allow him to relieve himself properly. He was covered in dried feces and urine. His legs and backside are rashy and infected because of it.'

'Sounds almighty miserable.'

'This isn't a joke, Mr. Balum. People have constitutional rights. You've violated them. You should take a look at his chest. It's covered in saddle sores, the skin rubbed raw, blistered and burning. Do you have any idea what that feels like?'

'Any idea what that feels like?' Balum's voice came out harsh and ragged, giving the young Marshal a jolt. 'Take another reading through that deposition I just gave you. Ask yourself what it feels like to be gunned down by a maniac with a gatling gun. Chased across fields in the frozen mountains half naked and worried, members of your family shot and killed, others maimed and wounded, all the while knowing your death is waiting for you up the trail. Ask yourself what that feels like, son, and then tell me about Mr. Nelson's rights.'

'This is a matter of law, Mr. Balum,' Freed fumbled the words out.

'Look boy,' Balum interrupted. 'Whatever pretty life you lived back East is only a fairytale out here. You've had your nose buried in law books, and that's fine. The law has to run its course. But this is the West. It takes a thicker skin than what you've grown to survive out here. Do I give a damn about his hunger and his goddamn saddle sores? I sure as hell don't. I could have shot him out there in the wilderness but I did my part and I brought him in so you could try him in your court of law. And that's as far as I'll go. From here on out you do with him as you please, and if you want to baby him and wipe his ass you go right ahead. He's in your hands now. I leave today. I'm done with it. But I'll tell you this, if I find out that man doesn't die at the end of a rope then I'll track him down and put a bullet through his skull.'

Balum's eyes pierced through the young man across the desk. He flashed a look to Buckling, who had long since dropped the newspaper and sat taking in the scene, then turned back to Johnny Freed.

'You think on that,' he said, then turned for the door.

Behind him Freed's voice whistled out. 'Hold it, Balum.'

Balum turned, his hand already at the door.

'You'll be going nowhere. Nelson's trial isn't scheduled for another two weeks and you're a key witness.'

'What the hell are you talking about? I just gave you the deposition.'

'As you should have. But your physical presence is required in court. I'll be issuing you a summons, and if you choose to disobey it I'll have Buckling here round up a posse and drag you in the same way you dragged in

Nelson.'

Balum turned to Buckling.

The Sheriff raised his hands slightly. 'It's the first I've heard about it,' he mumbled.

'You'd take me in?'

Buckling let his shoulders rise up in a show of powerlessness. 'Freed here is the new Marshal in the territory. If he gives me an order I don't have much choice but to follow up on it. Sorry, Balum.'

Balum turned back to the narrow-faced Marshal safe on the other side of the desk. The slender jaw clenched up in a show of resoluteness. Their eyes met and held for a moment longer than was comfortable to any three men in the room, until Balum turned on his heel and opened the door.

'You think on *that*, Balum,' came the young Marshal's voice.

The words hit Balum's back, sending hackles up his neck. He felt a fury rise in his throat, and pushed it down. His feet took him out of the jail office and he let the door slam shut behind him.

The two men plying their trade over matching chairs in the well-mirrored barber shop on Dade Street displayed coiffures cut to exact dimensions and matted down with a layer of pomade thick enough to make them shine nearly as cleanly as the mirrors along the walls. Each sported a part down the side of their crowns straight enough and deep enough that one could roll a quarter eagle down them, should he choose.

In one of those chairs, under the scissors of one of those barbers, sat Balum. His boots braced against the footrest and his eyes gazed upon the wood-beamed ceiling while the shearing sounds of scissor blades whisked overhead. He allowed the barber to apply a hot towel then cream to his face and, finally, the blade, thin and sharp and rasping in short strokes as the beard was removed and the smooth skin underneath revealed.

He felt his heart gradually return to calm as the barber worked above him. The gossiping from the men loitering in the shop resembled a ladies social hour. They spoke of commerce, new trades rising up in the area, the cattle business, and the train robberies that had occurred outside of Cheyenne.

In Denver, where their own railroad was growing, the arrival of the steam engine at the central station saw over a hundred new souls amble down from the train cars each week. It stretched the city's capacity until it popped and overflowed, and new streets were thrown down and buildings slapped together in a fortnight.

Everything was growing, thought Balum. And here he was, stagnant like a fish in a drying puddle.

The barber wiped the last bits of cream from Balum's face and untied the apron from around his neck. Balum stood and caught himself in the mirror. The image gave him a start. It had been a long time since he'd seen his face.

Tanned dark by the sun, it was wide and strong and older now. Older and alone, and trapped in Denver.

He looked away, annoyed at himself for allowing his mind to ruminate on the darker side of things. He needed distraction. The barber took his money, and his tip, and Balum left the old men in the shop to continue their gossip in the haze of cigar smoke.

In the street again under the heat of the sun, the urge came upon him to let his worries disappear in the flesh of a woman. The Baltimore Club tempted him, only a few blocks away. A feeling rose up in him, an urge to be sated by a woman, and he fought it, knowing full well where it would lead. The feelings had not yet left him, memories of the visions under the stars, the Shoshone's face. The awakening, as he had come to think of it.

It occurred to him he might partake in a game of poker. Anything to distract him. Maybe a glass of whiskey. Yet underneath all those fancies he knew they would not lead to lasting relief. He felt his anger rise again at Johnny Freed. A kid barely old enough to grow whiskers off his upper lip, toying with Balum like a marionette.

The idea of the Baltimore Club came back again and he shook his head, desperate for relief.

As if in answer to his perturbation, the world granted him a redirection. On the boardwalk running along the opposite side of the street walked a man with a long thick mane of black hair, his clothing fine and tailored and hinting at an education refined and deepened by culture.

Mr. Daniel Randolph. Philosopher, theater critic, lover

of life, as the man described himself. Balum felt a smile crease his face on remembering his first encounter with the man in a poker room not far from where he stood now.

'Daniel!' he shouted with his hand raised. Dodging horses and wagons, he crossed the street.

'Back so soon?' said Randolph with a firm grip on Balum's hand.

'Seems I can't stay away from Denver.'

'Plenty of catching up to do, friend.'

'That'll suit me. I need to take my mind off things.'

'The world's decided to trouble you?'

'It's thrown me a bronc I'm having trouble breaking.'

'Tell me.'

Right there in the shade of an awning outside a cluttered hardware store, Balum poured out his worries. He summed up the result of the Oregon Expedition, the vision, his awakening, and his current situation with the new Marshal.

'It's a handful,' said Randolph when the last of the story had come out.

'That it is.'

'More than anything else you want to find yourself a woman. Someone you love.'

'I do.'

Randolph eyed him from head to toe. 'You've gotten a good start there with a shave and a haircut. But by God do you look a sight from the neck down. Just look at yourself.'

Balum dropped his chin and took a look at his outfit. A ragged sight it was. His shirt was stained in sweat, dirty and threadbare. He wore old trousers, worn down from years of hard work. His boots were worn down at the heel and scuffed and dented in the toes. Around his hips was slung a gunbelt with a Colt Dragoon revolver in the holster, the only part of his makeup that appeared to be well cared for.

'When I met you,' said Randolph, 'you didn't have more than a few dollars to your name. But those cattle you boys brought out of Mexico made you rich. You want to take your mind off things? Let's spend some of that money and get you set up proper.'

Balum didn't argue. He followed Randolph's lead down the boardwalk, past the banking district, around the hotels and general stores and coming finally to a narrow business tucked between two large fabric shops. A sign advertising the services of a tailor was carved in wood and hung from rope over the entryway.

The man inside worked in a silent fashion, surrounded by reams of fabric and clothing hung in a chaotic yet somehow orderly manner. He measured the arms and neck and chest and inseam, around the waist and ankles, scratching figures into a small notebook at his side all the while. When he had finished he looked over his spectacles and insisted Balum not leave the shop without at least purchasing a readymade shirt and pants in order to lend a halfway respectable appearance during the few days required to tailor his suit. Randolph concurred with the suggestion and when they stepped back out onto the street, Balum's image, save for his boots, hat, and gunbelt, bore no resemblance to the savage looking beast that had arrived to town the day before.

In the street again, Balum replaced his hat. 'Where to now?' he asked.

'I'm going to have to keep you occupied all day, aren't I?'

'That's about the long and short of it.'

'Happy to do so. Fancy a game of faro?'

Balum hesitated.

'Poker?' ventured Randolph.

'As much as I'd like to, I'm afraid I'd lose all my money. My mind isn't in it.'

'There's a bit of a tournament at the Silver Nest tonight. Chester gave me the impression he'd like to throw his hat in.'

'Chester knows cards.'

'You fancy watching? As a spectator, nothing more.'

Balum slapped the long haired man on the back and grinned. 'Lead the way.'

The Silver Nest offered two levels; the lower for amateurs, the upper for high stakes players. At the bottom of the stairs Randolph paid for the both of them and they ascended into a room crowded with tables and chairs and gamblers dressed up for the occasion, each last one of them nervous, desperate with the hopes that their dreams might be met in short time, and their worries swept away like a spider at the end of a broomstick.

Chester's short frame mixed within them. They found him, and their presence brought a light to his eyes.

'I see I've got my boys in my corner,' he said.

'Of course you do,' said Balum. 'I'm surprised you didn't mention this last night.'

Chester scratched his neck, then let his thoughts be known. 'I figured it best not to. You're mind is heavy with other things. And, well... we've all seen you play poker, Balum, and no offense, it's worse than listening to a cat howl in the night. Tell me you aren't buying in.'

'Ha. Spoken as an honest friend. Don't worry, Chester. I'm only a spectator tonight.'

The gamesmaster rang a bell and called the hall to order. Players took their assigned seats, the dealing began, and Balum and Randolph relaxed with a drink behind their friend. It began well. Chester's chips began to stack up. As the cards were dealt, Chester would turn up the edges to allow the two men behind him a peak at what he was working with. An hour in, his luck turned and his chips went with it. They dwindled, and as they did, Balum felt a pressure rise within him, his breath tight and his thoughts far from his own concerns. He rode on the back of Chester's emotions as if it were his own money on the line, and when Chester's luck recovered on a flush and he raked in a pot overflowing with chips, Balum and Randolph could scarce keep themselves from dancing drunkenly behind him.

Hours passed in a tense pendulum between rejoice and despair. Liquor accompanied the rise and fall of emotion, and as the crowd intoxicated themselves with drink they erupted in gasps and cheers while the players sorted themselves into the victorious and the defeated.

When the gamesmaster rang the bell and called an end to the tournament, Chester found himself a richer man by a factor of ten. His old eyes turned to his friends, wide and reckless, and he demanded a round for the three of them.

They drank until their feet floundered below them. The heights of celebration, seldom disappointing, stoked the joy in Chester like a drywood fire doused in kerosene. His jubilation would find its apex in only one place; the Baltimore Club, and when the thought struck him he blurted it out with a passionate plea that his friends accompany him to continue the mania.

In a show of self-control more resolute than he was accustomed to, Balum declined. Chester's crestfallen face nearly swayed him back into the revelry, but Randolph interjected by reminding the old man of Balum's delicate frame of mind.

In the street they parted ways. Balum stumbled back to the hotel, up the stairs, through the door. On the floor, slipped under the door, was an envelope with Balum's name hand written in black ink. He ripped it open. The court summons. His drunken eyes struggled to make it out, and finally he threw it back to the floor and flopped onto the bed. From a reclined position he tossed his hat to the desk and pried his boots off with his toes.

For as drunk as he was, sleep would not take him.

With Chester and Randolph gone, the more pressing issues of his predicament came swarming back. Johnny

Freed's voice sounded in his mind. The image of Angelique, Nelson, the pending court date. His loneliness. As for what he would do when the trial was over, not a single notion did he have. Only emptiness.

He lay staring into the dim outlines of the room for some time. Moonlight illuminated the curtains over the window, and periodically he would hear the sounds of drunks in the street, hollering and screeching in all extremes of passion. He wondered if any were Chester's or Daniel's, until finally his mind relented and sleep overtook him.

# 5

Habits began.

Breakfast and coffee in the morning at the cafe across from the hotel. Shower and shave. Read the morning paper. Check the post office to see if Will's wedding invitation had arrived. Walk.

It wasn't much.

Some days he would saddle the roan and ride without direction. In the afternoons he would meet with Chester and Randolph and pass away the hours in conversation. The thought occurred to him on nearly a daily basis to take a walk to the seedier side of town where brothels outnumbered saloons and where women would call from doorways with painted faces and sweet smelling skin. The desire was great but his resolve proved greater, and he pushed the urges back.

He drank little. Only when the questions of what he would do with his life rose in his mind sharp and roaring, him without answer, would he throw back the whiskey, wondering fruitlessly if the answers might be found at the bottom of a glass. On those few nights of despair he would choose the same Mexican cantina he had discovered with

Chester. He enjoyed the darkness, the dirt floor, the soft murmur of Spanish and the serenity of an establishment without fanfare.

It was in the cantina, seated at a corner table the afternoon prior to the trial, that Chester gave him the news.

The old man came in gingerly, letting his eyes adjust to the dark and hoping to find Balum there, for he felt, perhaps unjustly, that his presence in the cantina was only permitted in the company of one who spoke the language. He paused inside the door. The barkeep looked a moment at him and with his eyes signaled to the corner. Chester turned. A minute later he was seated in the gloom with his friend, a glass of pulque before him.

He took a sip and moved his tongue over his lips as if something foreign was stuck to them.

'What the heck are we drinking, Balum?'

'Pulque. It'll make you strong.'

'Will it make me drunk?'

'If you drink enough of it.'

Chester considered for a moment, eyes staring at the thick sludge in the glass, then took a long slam of it.

'Thataboy, Chester.'

'Not so bad I guess. You sure it'll get me drunk?'

'I'm sure.'

'Good. You drunk yet?'

'No. Trial starts tomorrow. It'll be bad enough in a fresh state of mind, let alone hungover.'

'Good. Because there's something you need to know

and you won't want to be drunk when you hear it.'

Balum set his glass aside and leaned in.

'You said you killed Saul Farro?' said Chester.

'Not me. I saw him get shot and flung down a crevice. He must have fallen two hundred feet. Why do you ask?'

'Talk of the town is that he's about. Came in this morning.'

Balum stared blankly across the table for a minute. 'That's impossible.'

'It's what they're saying is all.'

'No way he could have survived that fall.'

'It'd pay to keep an eye out. You shooting his brother and all, why, if it is true he'll be looking to tally things up. You can guarantee yourself that.'

Balum shoved his chair back over the dirt floor and stood.

'Hey, where you going, Balum?'

'I need to see the Sheriff.'

'Don't leave me here,' Chester said, and gulped down the last of the pulque like a man led to a glacier mountain after endless days in the desert.

Balum crossed town in as straight a line as possible. Wagons reared to a stop in the street as he bolted obliviously across throughways. He marched through the dust in long strides, Chester running after him.

They arrived at the jail in the same moment as Ross Buckling. The Sheriff was coming up along the boardwalk with his hand half dragging and half supporting a young drunk man with no hat and blood streaked across his face from a broken nose. Blood dripped down the man's lips and chin and onto his sweat-stained shirt.

'Rowdiness starting early today, Ross?' said Balum, as the two groups met at the door.

'Seems like it gets earlier every week. Or maybe I'm just getting old.'

Ross pulled the man into the jail office and led him back into the cell block. Balum and Chester waited in the office.

'That boy's a fighter, I'll give him that,' said Ross when he came back through. 'That boy's nose has been broke more times than I can count. Seems that'd be punishment enough, but it don't hurt to add a little cell time to it.'

'You throw him in there with Nelson?' asked Balum.

'No. Nelson's an ornery son of a bitch. I keep him in a cell to himself. You come to check up on him? He's had enough visitors you'd think he was a damn politician.'

The comment was lost on Balum. He shook his head. 'I came to ask about Saul Farro. People are saying he's in town. You know anything about that?'

'I do,' Ross nodded. 'I surely do. He was here not but two hours ago.'

'Here?'

'Right here. Came in to pay his buddy a visit.'

Balum paced the short distance between the two desks like a bull in a bucking chute.

'Johnny was sitting at his desk when he come in,' continued the Sheriff. 'Saul sure got him worked up. He gave the Marshal some harebrained story, contradicted just

50

about everything you gave in your deposition, and I'll be damned if Johnny didn't take it hook line and sinker.'

'What did he say?'

'Oh I don't know, a bunch of horse shit. Makes you out to be one nasty fella.'

'Where's Freed now?'

'Up at the courthouse. You'd almost think he'd decided to go lawyering for Nelson. He told Saul he should testify in court, and he's been pushing the judge to set back the trial date for health reasons. Says Nelson still hasn't recovered, says he needs rest and recuperation.'

'Rest and recuperation?'

'Hell if I know. I think he plain just doesn't cotton to you, Balum. Don't ask me why. Some folks just rub each other the wrong way, I guess. But Johnny, he's done gone and taken sides. And it ain't yours. Every time Nelson's lawyer comes in, why Johnny jumps up and plays handmaid to him. Eager to help out any way he can.'

'Nelson has a lawyer?'

'Where you been these past two weeks, Balum? You ain't heard about his lawyer?'

'Haven't heard a thing.'

'Some highfalutin fatman. Expensive. Arrived last week by train. And Nelson didn't even send for him, that's what I can't figure. The man just showed up. Goes by the name of Crenshaw. Douglas Crenshaw.'

'Never heard of him,' said Balum.

'From Kansas City, apparently. He knows his business. You can see it when he talks.'

Chester listened, propped against the jail office door, mildly buzzed from the pulque. When the door opened suddenly behind him it sent him sprawling to the floor.

'What's all this?' said Johnny Freed, frowning at the old man picking himself off the ground. He turned to Balum. 'You've got a lot to answer for.'

'I've got plenty of questions myself,' replied Balum.

'I'll start with one. How many lies did you tell me in that deposition?'

'Lies?'

'You said Saul Farro was dead. Unless you can explain to me how a deadman is walking around town, I call that a lie.'

Balum's boot smacked the floorboards as he took a step toward the Marshal.

'Whoa now,' Ross Buckling moved in and put a hand between them. 'Easy now, Johnny.'

'I'm not wrong,' the Marshal defended himself.

'Everything I told you in that deposition was the truth as I saw it,' said Balum. 'Saul Farro was shot and thrown off a cliff. I considered him dead and that's what I told you. If he's alive it's not because I lied, but because of pure dumb luck. Don't go throwing that word around lightly, Johnny. A man's word is all he's got out here. And my word is good. I can be mistaken, but I'm no liar. Plenty of men have been shot for what you just said. You're in the West now, and you'd better wise up or you'll end up opening that mouth of yours when you'd have been better off keeping it shut.'

'Are you threatening a U.S. Marshal?'

'I'm giving you advice. You're young, you've grown up in a sheltered world, and you've got a nice big badge you think gives you the right to go spouting off,' Balum's eyes looked at the young man in front of him. 'It doesn't. You question my word again and the very least you'll get is your teeth knocked out of that pissy little face of yours.'

'It won't be me questioning you, Balum. You'll have to answer under oath. When the witnesses start talking, Nelson won't be the only one on trial.'

'What witnesses?'

'Saul Farro, for one. And I've agreed to testify on behalf of the defense. The state of Frederick Nelson when you brought him in was unacceptable. You mistreated a prisoner and your stories are falling apart under closer scrutiny. I aim to find out what happened out there with that wagon train. It's my sworn duty to do so. If a jury finds Nelson innocent, as I'm starting to suspect, we'll put you on trial and I'll be more than happy to see you swing from a rope myself if you're found guilty.'

'You're a goddamn fool,' Balum's rage spilled over. 'Saul Farro should be tried along with Nelson, not put up on display as a witness to the defense. He helped murder those people; he was in on it from the beginning.'

'You're quick to accuse a man, Balum. I prefer to let the judicial branch of government provide that verdict. Now kindly leave this office.'

# 6

'You should eat something, Balum,' Chester said, munching on creamed corn and steak. 'It'll do you good. Get your strength up.'

They sat in the restaurant attached to the Berlamont Hotel. Balum rested his elbows on the table with a hand over his neck and dug his fingers into the cords of rope-like muscle stretching from the base of his neck down through his back and shoulders.

'I can't eat,' he said.

'Man needs to eat.'

'I should have shot him out there in the wilderness and let the wolves pick at his body.'

'Why didn't you?'

'Those on the expedition wanted to see justice done right. Easterners, Chester. Can't understand them. Just look at that boy strutting around town calling himself a U.S. Marshal. A nice education he's been given in the schoolhouse, but where has it gotten him? The kid is dumb as a rock.'

'He's got you all worked up,' Chester licked grease from his fingers.

'Talking about putting me on trial...,' Balum winced as he turned his neck.

'Hey look,' Chester pointed with his fork toward the street. 'Randolph's on the loose.'

He jumped from his chair and scuttled outside. Balum watched from his seat, squeezing the soreness in his neck with his thick hand. The two talked outside briefly, then entered the restaurant.

'Pull up a chair, Daniel,' said Balum.

'Chester tells me this whole deal with Nelson is getting all fouled up.'

'More than fouled up,' said Balum. He gripped the table edge with one hand and his neck with the other and laid out the events from the previous two hours. More than once he took a long breath in and a long exhale out, and more than once did he grimace as pain shot through his neck.

'You wouldn't think it could get any worse,' said Randolph. 'Put *you* on trial?'

'The kid's just talking,' said Balum.

'He's needling you. What's wrong with your neck?'

Balum shook his head slightly. 'Feels like a knife is wedged in it.'

'You need to take care of that.'

'It's stress, that's all.'

'Baltimore Club,' said Chester. 'Nothing relieves stress like a woman.'

'Ah, what the hell,' said Balum. 'Let's go.'

'Really?' The old man's face lit up and he put his fork

down. Before Balum could respond, Randolph cut it.

'You're going to be sitting down all day tomorrow. If you want that neck worked on, I know the place to go, and it's not the Baltimore Club.'

'I need my mind off things, that's all I know,' said Balum.

'All right, gentlemen,' said Randolph. 'I'll lead the way.'

As was the reality of most towns, Denver had divided itself up into neighborhoods, districts, and *barrios*, each peculiar unto itself and each under endless metamorphoses as they were built and destroyed and raised again over time. The center of town belonged to banks and lending offices. Hotels had their strip, as did general stores, feed stores, confectioneries, blacksmiths and carpenters. Churches vied for worshipers, brothels fought for johns, and saloons competed for their drunks.

Not only was it divided along lines of business, but along ethnic and cultural lines as well. The Mexican cantina on the edge of town was neighbored by a Mexican grocer, the huts and shacks on the dusty streets built and inhabited by hard working Hispanics. Blacks, some long since escaped from southern slavery, others recently freed, lived not but a stone's throw from the Asian alleyways, the very architecture of the edifices beautiful and foreign to the eyes of the whites.

Daniel Randolph, a man of uncertain complexion, took advantage of his makeup. By keeping quiet he could walk the streets of nearly any district, a silent interloper seeking thrill in the limitless pleasure of each culture's eccentricities.

Out from the center of town he led them. Into narrow streets overflowing with vendors and pushcarts, stalls of produce and criers hollering out the sale of their wares in musical tongues. Strange clothing, hats unseen before, herbs and vegetables unnamable and foreign swarmed around them. Signs over storefronts lost their Latin alphabet, letters disappeared and morphed into characters of whose meaning Balum knew not what.

In a muddied street strung with red lanterns they drew to a stop before a door. A viewing hole slid open at Randolph's knock, a brief word was exchanged, and the door opened. A woman dressed in silk and a painted face greeted them in a candlelit room draped in soft-colored tones. Daniel did the talking and the three were led to separate rooms in back.

The interior of Balum's room was dark and furnished with plush fittings. Lantern light flickered under the shade of a painted globe. A table with a mattress over it made up the centerpiece. At the end of the mattress was a hole cut out for the comfort of one's face. He stood for a moment, unsure what to do, when the woman who had greeted them entered and, in broken English, made him understand that he was to disrobe and lie on the mattress.

The door closed and he wondered for a moment if he

had misunderstood her. If he had, he thought to himself, he would discover it soon enough. He pulled off his boots, his hat, the gunbelt and all the rest and laid them out over a chair then climbed onto the mattress where he covered his naked rump with a small towel and waited with his eyes closed.

In short order the door opened and closed and he felt the presence of a woman at his side. He felt his heart beat faster. He felt vulnerable, without control.

A drop of moisture touched his back and he flinched, then relaxed as warm hands began to rub the hot oil into the skin of his posterior. He felt pressure move to his neck, gentle squeezes, the press of thumbs and fingers. He felt the ropes of his muscle fight, then give in and relax in submission.

He let her take his arms and rub them down, his thighs, his calves, his feet and toes. She let her hands go from him, and a moment later he felt hot stones on his back. His throat let out a moan as she drew them over his body. The fascia below the skin relented, his mind fell into a trance. The stones were removed and the woman climbed onto the mattress and straddled his backside. Her hands ran along his spine, over his ribs and neck and shoulders, and he shuddered as previously unimaginable relaxation took hold of him.

She dismounted and he heard her voice for the first time, different from the matron's, yet no less exotic. She had him turn over, and as he did so she moved the towel over his crotch.

His eyes found her face in the dark. Hair as black as onyx gemstone swirled in pinned coils over her head. Her eyes were shadowed by thin lines of black paint, her lips red and full. She smiled at him and poured more oil over his chest. He watched her rub out the knots buried in his arms and chest, his legs. She stood behind his head and pressed her fingers delicately into his temples and his jaw, and pulled gently at his ears.

When she came back into view she had let the sash holding her robe go free and it opened, revealing two firm breasts and delicate nipples in the soft lantern light. She placed her hands on his chest and lightly ran them down his stomach to the towel covering his rising erection. She looked him in the eye with a smile, then bent and kissed his cheek as her hand crept below the towel and took hold of his throbbing shaft. She drew back from him, stroking gently with her oiled palm, and he raised an arm and put a hand to her breasts, fondling them as she massaged his cock in long smooth strokes. Her hand was warm and soft, it's rhythm unparalleled. At the end of each stroke she would give the head of his cock a twist, squeezing slightly, working the shaft faster and faster until he could take it no more and he erupted in a moan, his hand clutched tightly at her breast.

She brought a towel to him, cleaned him, cast the towel away. With more oil she drew her hands over the length of his body, massaging calm back into his frame. She kneaded the bundles of fibrous muscle until they were pliable once more and, when his body lay like a sleeping ragdoll, she gave him a gentle kiss on the cheek and departed.

# 7

The courthouse, such as they called it, had not kept pace with the developments racing throughout the rest of Denver. A one-storied hall, long and narrow and with a facade in need of a wash, brimmed with more people than it could possibly carry. They overflowed into the street, men and women cramming forward to catch a glimpse of Frederick Nelson as he was led from the jail to the courthouse by Sheriff Ross Buckling.

They had come from as far as Cheyenne, a hundred miles just to watch the show. A trial of such magnitude was a rare occurrence, and it served more than a cause for justice; it offered entertainment. Bets had been laid, a thousand arguments deliberated upon by the old men smoking cigars in the barbershop. Schoolchildren pretended they were Frederick Nelson in the playground, shooting their stick gatling guns at their playmates. Pastors decried the sordid story from the pulpit, proclaiming the judgment of heaven and laying out the punishment awaiting the man in hell. Every soul from Denver and beyond had an opinion of the affair, and their viewpoints were shouted at each other in a raucous chorus that came close to resembling a lynch mob on the morning of the first day of trial.

Into the fray Balum wedged himself. He wore his tailored suit for the first time, set off by a new pair of boots still stiff in the toes. Shoulders bumped him. He turned and squeezed through. The courthouse clerks saw him from the double doors and called out for the crowd to move back, yet they pushed forward like a herd of ants on an unrelenting mission. His size was what won out. He stood several inches taller than most men and had a wide set of shoulders laden with beef built by years of hard labor. Once inside he was escorted to the row behind the prosecution's bench where Ross Buckling had already taken up a position.

'If they don't convict him here, the mob outside'll get him,' said Balum, taking his seat.

'It's a rabble, alright,' said the Sheriff.

'Aren't you supposed to be out there laying down law and order?'

'I probably should be,' Ross grinned and squinted his eyes at Balum. 'Not in a pig's eye am I gonna miss this though.'

Settled into place, Balum took in his surroundings. In front of the hall on a raised platform gleamed the empty judge's chair. The twelve jury members sat in two rows along the side wall facing the court. Just in front of Balum was the prosecution bench, a table before it with papers stacked in a pile on top and the District Attorney seated alone.

On the other side of the aisle was gathered the defense. Balum let his eyes slide over. The fat lawyer brought in for the occasion reclined in his seat with his hands folded over his portly belly. He wore a fine suit with shiny buttons and a silver tipped bolo tie with an engraved clasp also hewn from sliver. Beside him sat Frederick Nelson with his hands manacled and his feet fettered at the ankles. An armed court bailiff stood behind him.

Behind Nelson, in the row corresponding to Balum's on the opposite side of the aisle, Saul Farro sat with a smile, his head turned toward Balum. He wore the appearance of a man quite pleased with himself. As though he found himself precisely where he most desired to be, the situation in accordance with his choosing.

Balum's eyes flashed to Nelson. The shackled felon gave off no sense of worry. On the contrary, his carriage portrayed a man mildly impatient and in total confidence of his stature, as if the courtroom was his own, the assembled crowd waiting to fulfill his bidding.

'Nelson looks too calm,' said Balum.

'It's just a show,' said Ross. 'He's shaking inside.'

'Where's Freed?'

'In the back there,' Ross tilted his head back toward the double doors.

'What's that lawyers name again?'

'Douglas Crenshaw.'

'Looks fancy.'

'He is fancy. Fancier than what Nelson deserves.'

Balum brought a hand up to his jaw and ran it across

the smooth-shaven skin. He felt the worry rise up in him again, and brought a hand to his neck but the pain had not returned.

A door to the side of the jury opened and a bailiff standing in front of the court called out for all to rise for the honorable Judge Vanderloop. The audience rose, the judge took his seat, and court came to session.

Court proceedings, Balum soon discovered, did not move smoothly or efficiently. Legal jargon was bandied about, phrases recited and repeated, the lawyers taking turns to ramble on about prior cases and precedents set. Balum felt his mind go numb and his legs get restless. He wished he was outside in the sunshine with a plug of tobacco in his cheek. Anywhere but stuck in the stuffy courtroom with the smell of an overfilled house of people sweating and stinking in a ventless chamber. He'd prefer to be sitting in the Mexican cantina with a glass of mezcal and the banter of Chester and Randolph giving him reason to laugh.

He took another glance behind him at the assembled body and searched out his friends within it. Their faces were not to be found. Only Johnny Freed, standing in back at the double doors with his arms crossed over his narrow chest and his face pouting and foolish.

Balum felt his neck twitch and he swung back around to face the front. As he turned, his eyes flowed unfocused across the rows of seated onlookers and, suddenly, like a horse startled by a snake, his head jerked to a stop and he stared across the aisle and behind him at unexpected beauty.

She caught him looking and held his eyes in hers for a moment that lasted no more than a few seconds, but felt to Balum an eternity all unto itself. Her features were fine and delicate, her mouth set firmly and her eyes stern and piercing. Light brown hair flowed in shimmering waves down her back, and the blue dress she wore covered a frame that drew the focus of every man that happened to set eyes on it. She reminded him briefly of Deborah DeLace; the set of her mouth and the petite yet powerful body of a woman sleek and tempting.

He nudged Ross next to him and whispered to him, 'Who's that girl over there? In the blue dress.'

Ross looked over and whispered back to Balum, 'Sara Sanderson. Aston Sanderson's daughter.'

'Who's Aston Sanderson?'

'Eastern money.'

'What's that mean?'

Ross shrugged and gave a shake of his head.

Balum looked over again but the girl sat facing forward with her eyes firmly on the proceedings taking place at the front of the court. Balum felt a knot of pressure rise in his chest. He felt certain that though her eyes faced forward she nonetheless watched him from her periphery.

He forced himself to turn and face the front, though try as he might he could not bring himself to focus on the opening motions of the trial no matter how hard he bent his mind. The lawyers rambled on about matters strange and distant to him, and he sat rigidly on the bench with his jaw set, waiting for the afternoon recess and knowing where his mind was leading him, for he was old enough to know himself, and recognized the familiar cudgel that hijacked his senses, wielded only by the rarest of women; women to which he had yet found no riposte.

By the time the noon recess arrived, opening arguments had still not been made. The assembled crowd filed out of the hall and into the Denver avenues, gossiping and carrying on and complaining that not enough excitement had happened.

In the streets Balum asked Ross Buckling again about the girl from the courtroom and her family.

'What do you mean by Eastern money?' he asked.

'I mean they come out here from Kansas City and they got money. At least, that's what it looks like to me. He floats around with the business crowd. Bankers and such. Not sure exactly what his trade is.'

'That's hardly the East.'

'Close enough.'

'How long have they been out here?'

'A few months is all. And she's caught about every man's eye in the state. Johnny Freed's included.'

'Is that right?'

'That boy is smitten. Talks about her like she's his bride-to-be. But the kid's a fool, anyone can see that. She don't pay him no mind. Looks at him like he's a dog with mange, but he keeps after her anyway.'

Balum didn't respond. He scanned the crowd, seeking

her out, and when he saw the blue dress down the street entering a restaurant he gave the Sheriff a slap on the arm.

'Care for lunch?'

'It's what the recess is for.'

Balum led the way to the dining hall. When Ross Buckling saw where they were headed he hesitated.

'A little pricey for me, Balum.'

But Balum had a mission. He pulled the Sheriff in, insisting lunch was on him, and they were soon seated at a table covered in white linen and topped with place settings numerous enough to confuse the both of them. They ordered off the menu and when Ross saw where Balum's focus had drifted, he followed the line of sight then turned and rolled his eyes.

'Now I see why we're here,' he said dryly.

'She's beautiful.'

'You sound like a schoolboy.'

'Maybe.'

'Well,' said Ross, 'you gonna go talk to her or sit here staring like Johnny would do?'

'We'll eat first. I figure I'll try some manners and not barge in on their meal. Is that Aston Sanderson there with her?'

Ross looked over. 'That's him. And Mrs. Sanderson.'

'He doesn't look like a banker. Looks a bit rough.'

'I didn't say he was. Just who he floats around with.'

They ate their meal and when they were finished Balum had still not made a move to introduce himself to the Sanderson's table.

'Cold feet, Balum?' Ross egged him on. 'Thought you was a ladies' man.'

'The trial's on my mind.'

'No it ain't. Ain't nothing on your mind but that gal there.'

The Sanderson table rose to leave and when they did Sara looked his way. Her eyes locked onto his again, and by her reaction he realized she had known he was there all along. At the door a blue kerchief matching her dress fell from her purse and landed softly on the floor. She left without it, and he jumped from the table and snatched it from the ground. Outside he jogged after her, and called out when he had nearly reached her.

'Ma'am,' he said.

She turned, her face composed as if she had been expecting him. Balum held out the kerchief.

'I believe you dropped this.'

'Why thank you,' she smiled and took it with a glove-covered hand.

'I saw you at the trial,' he said. 'The name's Balum.'

'I believe I saw you too,' she replied. 'I'm Sara Sanderson.'

'A pleasure to meet you. It was an unexpected surprise to see a woman such as yourself there.'

'It's a fascinating trial. I wouldn't miss it for the world.'

'I'd love to hear your thoughts on it.'

'Perhaps you will. You'll have to invite me out first, and I won't be dropping anymore kerchiefs to give you the easy opportunity.'

She turned sharply and left him standing dumbfounded in the street and feeling like a fool.

He returned to the restaurant and paid his bill while Ross Buckling picked at his teeth.

'That weren't no accident she dropped that kerchief,' he prodded. 'That gal knew you was watching her.'

'Maybe,' admitted Balum.

'Long line of muchachos waiting to court her. Maybe you just jumped to the front of it.'

They battled their way back through the throngs gathered at the courthouse doors and reclaimed their seats behind the District Attorney's bench. Judge Vanderloop entered, the attendants rose, and when seated again he thumped the gavel and brought the court to session.

After another stretch of time was wasted in legal speak, throughout which Balum could scarce put attention due to the overwhelming awareness of Sara Sanderson seated on the other side of the aisle. Saul Farro sat not far from her, throwing the occasional glare in Balum's direction, and Frederick Nelson leaned back in his chair alongside Crenshaw with a smug grin plastered over his face.

Through all of it the hint of a question arose in Balum's mind. Why were the Sandersons seated in the aisle behind the defense? But he shook it off. This wasn't a wedding ceremony. People took seats wherever they found them, and no one sitting behind the defense, aside from Saul Farro, put their endorsement there.

The District Attorney rose and gave his opening

statement. He spoke in succinct phrases, framing the case through dry and logical parameters. He gave a summary of the facts, the evidence, the case that the defense would be assumed to make. Each possible argument he rebutted before Crenshaw had a chance to articulate it.

When he'd finished he took his seat. Murmurs rose from the hall. Ross glanced at Balum and gave him a nod with his head, suggesting a vote of confidence in what they had just witnessed. Judge Vanderloop opened the floor to the defense.

Douglas Crenshaw lifted his fat body from the defense bench and sauntered into the open floor before the judge's chair, then turned to face the jury.

'Distinguished members of the jury,' he began. 'A crime has been committed, and it is your responsibility to find its perpetrator. But it is not the crime you think. Far from it. Let us consider. You have been told a massacre has happened. You have been led to believe that this poor man sitting in chains before you is a crazed murderer of innocent people. Yet where is the evidence? Where are these supposed bodies lying dead in the mountains? All we have is the word from a known drunkard, a gambler, and a prolific womanizer, appointed U.S. Deputy Marshal under suspicious pretenses, and not an ounce of shame does he carry with him before God. He abused my client, starving him and bringing him to custody replete with bodily injury. He's given over sheets of paper claiming to be affidavits from members of the Oregon Expedition, yet it is more than likely they have been forged by his own hand. His own deposition has been found to be full of lies and false innuendoes. That man, the real criminal here, sits in this courtroom today. His name is Balum, and he should be hung.'

A roar of chatter burst through the hall. Judge Vanderloop smacked his gavel over the sound block while the District Attorney shouted his objection. Silence was not so easily brought to the courthouse. The rabble whooped and shouted. From the opposite side of the aisle Saul Farro leaned forward and peered down the bench to where Balum sat, a look of revelry smeared across his face.

When the judge at last brought order to the hall he looked down from his seat and reprimanded Crenshaw. The public was not on trial, he admonished the defense lawyer. Crenshaw only nodded, unimpressed, and continued his dialogue.

'All of these things I say to you now will be presented to you in the coming days. Witnesses will testify on what I have just said. The truth shall come out and Frederick Nelson's innocence will be proven. I ask not for leniency, but for your good judgement. This is a farce, a complete lie, and zero, I repeat, zero evidence of wrongdoing has been carried out by my client. That is all.'

Another ripple of commotion went rushing through the hall. The benches were crammed with bodies. Those that couldn't fit in seats stood shoulder to shoulder in the hot courtroom air where they burst into discussion and argument. Not a one was put off by Crenshaw's flamboyant opening statement. On the contrary, it was what they had come for; entertainment. The man on trial was for the most part unknown to them. Balum, though he had previously lived in Denver for two months as Deputy Marshal, was nonetheless a near-unknown figure in town. Such men, nearly blank slates, were just the type of men the citizenry craved to cast under public scrutiny.

Judge Vanderloop shouted out his adjournment of the court and told the rabble that the hearing would resume at noon on the following day. Those who were seated jumped to their feet, the double doors swung open, and the court emptied.

# 8

Alone in the dark hotel room, Balum sat on the edge of the bed, hat hanging in his fingertips between his knees. His chin rested low on his chest and the soft flutter of wind broke at his window.

His friends had tried to console him. Chester bought him fine whiskey but he had no want to drink it. Randolph ordered food but his hunger had abandoned him. The encouragement they offered felt weak in the face of a justice system seemingly inside out and set against him. He'd sat in their company with a great bulge of tobacco in his cheek until night fell and he wandered back to the Berlamont Hotel alone, wearied further by the unrelenting awareness that Saul Farro walked the streets in total freedom.

They should have shot Nelson, he told himself again. Left his body as carrion for the vultures, his bones to be bleached over time by the sun in that desolate wilderness of endless sky where the only life was the call of the wolf in the shadows of dusk.

But that chance had passed.

When sleep finally took him it was only by thinking of

the one point of light in all his narrow vision; Sara Sanderson. He dreamt of her; the kerchief, her eyes intense and unafraid. Her image scrolled across the fields of his mind, easing him into slumber, but only for so long. Other images rose up. Frederick Nelson, Angelique, gatling guns, the Shoshone medicine man.

He woke in a sweat before the sun had climbed over the earth's rim. His chest was wet with perspiration. He rose and lit the lantern on the desk, then drew his Colt Dragoon revolver from its holster and disassembled it. With a rag he cleaned each part of the weapon, shining it and caring for it as one would a precious gemstone. He checked the rounds in the cylinder and put the gun back together and dropped it back in the gunbelt.

He dressed himself, left the hotel, and stepped into the dawn of the rising sun in time to watch it cast its first rays over empty dust-covered streets. Breakfast at the hotel restaurant sat well in his belly, washed down with several cups of black coffee strong enough to make his eyes bulge.

He had time to kill. The court docket was filled with minor cases. With only one courthouse, time had to be allocated to process them all. Drunks, horse thieves, cattle rustlers, and card sharks, they all needed their day in court. Frederick Nelson's hearing would not resume again until the afternoon. Until then, Balum needed distraction. For a moment he considered the massage parlor. A temptation, certainly, but one that lent only temporary respite.

A more meaningful pursuit awaited; Sara Sanderson.

With a fresh plug of tobacco in his cheek, he strolled

the boulevards, one eye open for the lady, the other tensed and waiting for Saul Farro.

It took not but two blocks to notice the difference from the days before. Until that morning, he was one man among thousands. Ordinary and unworthy of attention. In one day that had changed. Eyes flashed over him, stolen glances followed by hushed whispers. Women nudged their friends with their elbows and men pointed discreetly to their companions at the freshly-accused stranger now tangled completely into the drama of Frederick Nelson and the Oregon Expedition massacre. He could feel their judgement, sense their suspicion and doubt. New bets were being wagered, odds being struck as to who the real killer was, the real story, the truth.

Not a thing there was he could do about it. He walked forward, ignoring the gawkers, holding his head high and his shoulders back. His feet took him over the shaded boardwalks, across streets filled with traffic and lazy dogs and carts and buggies and all kinds of commotion particular to a city in flux. He spat tobacco into the street and sighed and wondered if he should return to the Berlamont Hotel and hold tight until trial time. The staring and gossiping his presence caused had begun to eat through him.

The urge had started to win over when he caught a glimpse of the two figures taking tea on the veranda of the Rendezvous Hotel. He turned sharply and felt his blood pump as his legs took great strides across the street. It wasn't the first time he'd looked up from the street to the raised veranda of the hotel to flirt with a woman, but this was different. It wasn't just a pretty girl like Leigha Atkisson, or a floozy like Suzanne Darrow. Sara Sanderson was something else entirely. There was something deeper that pulled him to her. Something hypnotic.

She sat at a small table with her mother, dressed immaculately and sipping tea as if she were in a London teahouse. As he approached he saw Mrs. Sanderson set her teacup down and rise and disappear through the hotel door. Sara sat alone, looking out over the street. Balum closed in and at the railing he removed his hat and smiled.

'A very fine morning, Ms. Sanderson.'

'Hello, Mr. Balum,' she said, her eyes watching him, amused.

'Does the Rendezvous serve a good tea?'

'It's passable.'

'I've never tried it myself.'

'Too busy bringing murderers to justice?'

'The courtroom might make it sound that way. Maybe I've just never had the right company to take tea with.'

'Is that an invitation? Or have you not worked up the nerve yet?'

Balum leaned back, knocked off balance by the abruptness. 'It was shaping up to be an invitation. Let me word it straightforward to you; I'd like to take you to tea. Right here, tomorrow morning.'

She looked down at him over the railing from her elevated position on the veranda. 'I doubt my father would approve. The courtroom makes you out to be more than an

76

arm of justice. The talk of the town is that it's all a made up story. You had some ax to grind with Nelson and the truth will soon come out.'

Balum slapped his hat against his thigh and spat. 'That lawyer Crenshaw is a piece of work. I've never heard such a load of nonsense. Nelson will hang by a rope, you'll see.'

'Perhaps. In the meantime, if you expect to court me you'll have to win over my father,' she paused, then gave a suggestive shrug of her shoulders, 'or chase me down when no one's the wiser.'

Balum watched her toss her hair over her shoulder. He knew she was toying with him. Her implication was at once unclear yet suggestive of something taboo. His mind worked to find a response, but had come up with nothing when Mrs. Sanderson reappeared from the hotel doorway.

'Oh, the talk of the town,' she said, taking the seat beside her daughter.

'Good afternoon, ma'am,' said Balum. 'The name's Balum.'

'I'm well aware. It's been on everyone's lips this morning. I'm Mary Sanderson. I assume you've met my daughter.'

'Yes ma'am. We were just chatting about the trial. It's too bad my name's being drug through it, but the facts will be clear in the end.'

'I'm sure they will,' she said. Her face betrayed nothing of the thoughts underneath.

'Speaking of which,' he said, 'I'll need to get going. It

starts up in an hour and I need to be present. Good day, ladies.' He replaced his hat and left them to their tea, retracing his steps away from the Rendezvous Hotel in a much more cheerful disposition than when he had first laid them down.

The courthouse was no less smothering than the day before. Those who had missed the opening day were rue to miss out on the gossip that might emerge from the second. The only person absent that Balum was quick to note was Ross Buckling. The Sheriff's duties could only be postponed for so long. His absence meant Balum sat alone on the bench. Neither Chester nor Randolph had been able to make it through the crowds out front. The bailiffs and court clerks ran it like a private club for the rich, and rumors had already started swirling that bribes were being handed out in exchange for admission.

After the customary rising and sitting when Judge Vanderloop entered, the court was called to order and the spectacle took up where it had left off. Residents of Denver who had dealt with Nelson before the Oregon Expedition departed were called to the stand. The owner of Jackson Stables, a wagon maker, and several who had been eager to join the expedition but who lacked the cash deposit all took the witness stand one by one after swearing on the bible and staring solemnly out into the hall as questions were put to them.

Frederick Nelson was a handsome man, well spoken when he wished to be. He exuded confidence and gave off an air of expertise in any conversation he took part in. He was a conman through and through, and being a man who excelled at his trade, had duped the townsfolk during his short stay in the city. Though the District Attorney brought up valid points about Nelson's choice of men, the mandatory fee to join the expedition, and doubts surrounding the only other expedition he led which ended in what was labeled an Indian attack, but of which there was no trace. To each of these points Douglas Crenshaw would rise and pace the small area in front of the jurors, dealing out simple questions that would elicit simple-minded answers, all of which only bolstered Nelson's credibility.

When Judge Vanderloop adjourned the court for the day with an announcement that the case would not resume until three days later, public opinion had only shifted in favor of Nelson's innocence.

Balum let himself fold into the crowd exiting the hall, ignoring Saul Farro's elated expression of schadenfreude across the aisle. Chester waited for him outside. Together they left the center of town for the quieter side where the Mexican cantina offered the comfort of its dark interior and clientele more indifferent to his predicament that anything else. They ate pozole and chiles rellenos with Chester lending encouragement all the while, only to land on deaf ears, for though the case against Nelson appeared more insubstantial by the hour, Balum's mind had space only for Sara Sanderson.

# 9

A cold morning. Dew on the windowsill.

Looking out at the night sky with his hands braced against the window ledge, he could not guess what hour it might be. Night had not left its hold over the land; morning waited patiently on the underbelly of earth.

He grabbed up his regular, more comfortable clothing, and dressed himself, knowing sleep would not return to him, then descended the stairs to an empty lobby and out the door. In the crisp air of the pre-dawn he stood motionless like a soldier awaiting orders, until the cold woke him and he turned and walked to the edge of town and watched the horses snort and sputter as they trotted the circumference of the livery corral. He stood watching, his thoughts nowhere, and when the sun rose and the sounds of the town's awakening reached him, he left the horses to their pacing and walked back to town.

He had nowhere to be after breakfast so he stood in front of the Berlamont Hotel with tobacco in his lip and watched the passersby. Their steps and the clomp of their horses raised dust through which the sun sent its rays. It illuminated the small clouds of dirt as they rose and plumed and wafted gently back to the ground. He watched ladies lift their skirts and men take their women's hands when descending from the boardwalks to the street. Their actions gave his mind allowance to think of Sara Sanderson, and just as it began to form the image of the young beauty, the woman herself appeared down the length of the street atop a paint horse.

Balum spat and wiped his lip and watched her ride forward, her eyes already on him from a hundred yards out. Like she knew where he'd be.

Abreast of the hotel she reigned in the horse and looked him over head to toe. He wore brown canvas pants and an old threadbare military shirt tucked under a battered canvas jacket. A leather gunbelt hung at his hips. Only the new boots, still bearing a shine, gave any sense of a man of wealth hidden behind the outfit.

'You look better in your tailored suit,' she said.

'That's a fine way to greet a man in the morning.'

'I speak my mind.'

'I see you do.'

She was dressed in ladies riding gear; a multi-layered calico riding skirt and a double breasted vest that clung tightly to her petite frame. A riding whip extended out from her hand, and she held it as though she enjoyed using it.

'I thought I'd take a ride today,' she said. 'Where would you suggest I go? I'd like to find a shaded spot where I can look out on fields of wildflowers.'

'Toward the foothills,' he raised an arm westward. 'It's

pretty out that way.'

'I'm sure it is. It's too bad I'm riding alone today; a pretty landscape is better appreciated by two.'

The forwardness of it struck him. She gave him all the openings while at the same time appearing aloof. He took his hat off and ran a hand through his hair.

'Safer that way too,' he said. 'Lot of wild men riding these parts.'

'I'm sure there are.'

'I'm of a mind to saddle up the roan and accompany you. If you'd accept the offer.'

She raised the riding whip slightly and peered down at him for a moment with her eyes laughing in the corners. 'From what I've heard in the courthouse, you might be precisely one of those wild men I should be wary of.'

She brought the whip down and the paint jumped forward, leaving Balum standing with his mouth half open and the passersby gossiping amongst themselves about what had just taken place. A decision was made in his mind, shot off like the blast of nitroglycerin in a mine shaft. He stepped into the street where the tracks of her paint had just stood, and let the contours of the hoof prints engrave themselves in his memory. His roan waited in the livery. It had been days since it had stretched its legs, and now it would have fair reason.

He turned on his heel in direction of the stables and nearly ran straight into the District Attorney.

'Balum,' started the pale-faced man. 'Do you have a free moment? I need to speak to you about the trial. You'll be called to the witness stand soon and I want you to be prepared for the questioning.'

Balum took a last look up the street at where Sara's figure was receding.

'Ah…,' he hesitated.

'This is important, Balum. Come, follow me to the courthouse. We have some items to go over.'

'Can it wait?'

'No it can't. I don't know when you'll be called to the stand, but it could be soon, and I want you ready.'

The attorney was right; there were more important things to do than chasing pretty girls over the foothills. Still, Balum knew there was only one place he would like to be. Instead he followed the spectacled man to an office in the courthouse biting his tongue all the while.

'I've never seen anything like it,' said the attorney when they had taken seats across the desk from one another. 'This Crenshaw fellow has got a list of witnesses from here to Sunday. He's got a notary expert that he's called in for handwriting analysis. I don't even know what that means. He's no ordinary lawyer. The man's done this before.'

'So where do I fit in?' asked Balum. 'I've given my deposition. What more do they need from me?'

'He's gonna needle you on that witness stand until you break. That's what he'll do. You said in the deposition that Saul Farro was dead, and it's clear he's alive and well. You've got the affidavits, but that's just paper. What it's coming down to is two men's word against one. You're the one. That means what you've got to say better be solid like a rock.'

'I should have shot him in the mountains.'

'Well, that opportunity is past us, so let's concentrate on what's at hand. Ready?'

They went over the events in detail. The attorney asked questions at every turn in the trail. Some questions were meant to find answers, others to give Balum a taste of what Crenshaw might dish out. By the time it was over, two full hours had disappeared and Balum's head felt like it had been fed through a grain mill. He left the courthouse with a hand shielding his eyes from the sun as though a convict released from an underground prison.

Hunger crawled up in his belly, but he knew it could wait. He directed himself to the livery and led the roan out from its stall, brushed him down, saddled him, and rode out through the back corral gates and turned toward the foothills.

The trails leading into town were a convolution of tracks from all kinds of beast; horse, mule, goat, cow, ox and donkey. There were wagon wheel ruts, those of carts and buggies and things drug behind animals. Human footprints mixed with those of chicken claws, and any other imprint the ground would hold it did.

Balum rode out until the commotion of prints dissipated and began to cut back and forth for sign of the paint. He found it, or what he guessed was her horse, a half mile out from the city. She was headed northwest, the snow-capped peaks of the Rockies far in the distance. He followed a ways, then lost the trail over hard ground, picked it up again, then found himself searching once more. A quarter of an hour was lost until he found where she had crossed a small stream. The paint's tracks were clear and unmistakable in the sand along the banks. When he lost the trail again he took a look into the distance and followed the most likely route. It worked. The paint's tracks showed up again, fresher. He was gaining ground.

Another half hour's ride and he caught a glimpse of a rider a few miles out. Just a dark speck in a meadow, nothing more. The roan accelerated its pace and soon he could make out the distinct spotting of the paint. The roan leaned itself forward into a canter and Balum leaned low across the horse's neck, the weight of his feet pressed into the stirrups, his head bent low so the brim of his hat would not catch the wind.

She saw him at a mile's distance and set her own horse to a run. When the gap began to close she brought the whip down on the paint's flank and the horse took off into a gallop. Balum gave the roan its head and the three beat canter turned to a four beat gallop, the wind whipping against him and sweat lathering across the horse's withers.

The chase was on. Through grass-covered fields, over small rises and plains of flowers reflecting brightly the force of the sun, they trammeled the earth in a frenzied sprint, horses snorting and hoofbeats crashing below their riders.

The paint was a good horse, healthy and young, but the roan was a beast like few others. It stood seventeen hands high and had thighs and shoulders laden with muscles made for just such a run. The two horses charged in wild-eyed conviction until the paint began to slow, its gait dropping back to a canter, and the roan, sensing its own victory, made a final push that brought it up on the paint's rear until Balum was near enough to reach out and slap the tiring horse's flank.

They slowed the horses, bringing them back to a walk. The animals' sides heaved and they shook their necks, throwing their manes wildly over the crests and raising and shaking their muzzles with snorts and nickers.

Under a grove of pitch pine they brought them to a stop and Sara turned to Balum with her cheeks flushed red and sweat glistening on her brow. His own heart drummed against his chest and he felt the rush of breath sucking in and out of him as the two looked into the eyes of one another.

'Well you've caught me,' she said. 'Now what do you plan to do with me?'

Before he could answer she spoke again.

'Will you take me and ravage me underneath the pines where no one will see you? Shall you rip me from my horse and throw me to the ground? Are you going to have your way with me, Mr. Balum? Is that the man you are?'

She said it not in fear, but nearly as an invitation. And he knew, very much so, that he was exactly such a man.

But Sara, her lips parted and hot, her breasts rising in deep breaths beneath her vest, was not such a woman. At least Balum did not believe so. Did not want to believe it. He swung from the saddle and let the reins drop to the ground. Circling around to her side he raised a hand to her and she took it and dismounted from the saddle.

'I'll save the ravaging for another day,' he said. 'Today I am a gentleman inviting a lady to sit in the shade of a pine stand and marvel at the beauty around us.'

She had a blanket with her and they spread it across the fallen pine needles and sat lounging while birds sang above them and a breeze bent the grass in a sea of flowing green. They talked of Denver, of Kansas City, of horses and ranching, and laid out their visions of what a home would look like built right there by the pine grove, with fields of junegrass and wildflowers blooming all around.

When they folded the blanket and took to the saddles again, the sun was only just beginning its decline onto the Rocky Mountains.

'You know,' said Sara, 'you can't go chasing me off into the foothills every time you wish to see me. You must come and meet my father and introduce yourself.'

'I plan on doing exactly that. Plan for me to come by tomorrow evening. Are you staying at the Rendezvous?'

'That was just for tea. We're on High Street. The house with the blue painted door. I'll tell my father to expect you.'

# 10

'Not a care in the world.'

'That's right, Chester. Not a care in the world.'

They sat in the cantina with a plate of nopales between them, Chester with a glass of homebrew beer and Balum with water drawn from the well.

'Sure you don't fancy a drink? Man ain't meant to drink whilst his friend sits and watches.'

'I'm sure. Need to be fresh for tomorrow.'

'That's all well and good, Balum. But truth is, you ain't in a position to be so carefree. You got a big plate set before ye and having gals on the mind only clouds it up.'

'This isn't just any girl.'

'I heard you. This one's different.' Chester poked at the nopales and made a face at the slime clinging to them. 'Fact is though, you only just met her, and in the state of mind you're in, why, you might let your heart get ahead of your better judgement.'

'What's that mean?'

'What's that mean? Why ever since you ate that sack of Shoshone medicine man voodoo you've been talking about all you want to do is settle down and marry a gal and stop cavorting with whores and loose women. Which, of course, I commend you for. But dang, Balum, that Crenshaw fellow is turning this whole case around and trying to pin something on you. You need your mind right.'

'My mind's as clear as ever, Chester.'

The old man brought a forkful of the drooly cactus dish to his mouth and chewed while making a face, then, as if having judged the nopales and found them worthy, hauled in two more quick mouthfuls.

'You say these Sandersons are from Kansas City?' he asked with his mouth full of cactus.

'That's right.'

'Isn't that where Nelson's lawyer is from? Crenshaw?'

Balum shrugged. 'Coincidence I guess.'

Chester took a slam of beer and leaned back. 'I reckon,' he mumbled.

Balum pushed back his chair. 'I'll leave you to it, Chester. Need my rest.'

'Hold on, hold, on, let me finish,' he downed the mug in three tremendous gulps and let the mug drop to the table. He shook his head and belched. 'Alright. Now we're ready.'

They parted ways at the Silver Nest, Chester convinced he'd win enough for a turn at the Baltimore Club, and Balum swung back to the Berlamont Hotel for his bed. In the lobby the receptionist flagged him down.

'Couple letters came for you, Balum. I slipped them under your door.'

He climbed the stairs, opened the door, and there they

were; two cream colored envelopes side by side on the hardwood floor. He bent and picked them up and read the writing on the back. Addressed to him. The letter on top from Will. A wedding invitation, no doubt.

He felt a tightness in his throat and an emptiness inside him when he saw the name of the sender on the second envelope. Angelique.

He slipped a finger through the flap and nearly ripped it open, then stopped, held it a moment, and set it carefully on the tabletop. Will's letter remained in his other hand and he opened it. An invitation, as he'd figured, the wedding to be held the following weekend. Balum frowned and checked the date of the letter. Two weeks past. A ten year old boy could deliver mail faster than that, he thought to himself. The question came to him of when Angelique's letter had been written, and how long it had been delayed in its delivery. The thought only brought the tightness back, the empty feeling in his belly. He undressed and forced his mind to go blank, for the rivalry of emotions within him was something foreign to him, and required a skill set which he knew he did not possess.

It was the first thing he saw when he woke. His eyes were drawn to it, the cream envelope sitting atop the desk, his name and Angelique's written so closely together.

He dressed and left the hotel. In a cafe across the street he took breakfast and coffee, then ambled down the avenues until he came to the barbershop. In a chair alongside the old men smoking cigars he sat, the gossip taking a pause before it could be bottled up no longer, and the intrigue of the trial poured out. The men in the shop gave him their encouragement. They told him they believed Nelson was a guilty man and that he would meet his justice, that all would be settled in the end. Balum took his turn in the chair and responded in short grunts as the straight razor scraped along his jaw and down his neck. With his face clean shaven and his hair cut straight again, he lunched alone in the same cafe as before and returned to the hotel. He wasted an undue amount of time in a bath, scrubbing under his nails and behind his ears, soaking in the warm bubbles and wondering if he would ever get used to the feeling of money.

In the late hours of the afternoon he stood at the mirror in his room and smoothed out the tailored suit over his frame. He combed his hair and gave his boots a polish, all the while aware of the sealed envelope sitting on the otherwise empty desk.

The figure on display when he left the hotel and walked up High Street was of nothing less than a gentleman. One with a rugged face, hands tanned and calloused from work, but clean cut and dressed in finery.

The house with the blue door stood at the far end of the street. One of the newer homes, it rose two stories off the ground and bore the victorian touches of the times. The type of home he'd never dreamt of setting foot in, Balum thought to himself as he rose his hand to the door and rapped at the solid wood piece.

When it swung open Aston Sanderson stood in the entranceway. A big man, impeccably dressed, tall and confident in a way that reminded Balum of Frederick Nelson.

'Mr. Balum,' he boomed, and extended his hand. 'I've been expecting you. Come in. Are you a whiskey man? I was just sampling some labels. Follow me.'

They crossed the sitting room, Balum a few steps behind his host, and entered the parlor where a ruddy-faced man several pounds in excess of what his frame should support stood pouring small drams into a row of glasses.

'Balum,' said Aston. 'Meet Shane Carly, whiskey distributor.'

'Try this,' Carly held out a glass containing a splash amber liquid in the bottom. 'This is the best rye whiskey you'll see west of the Mississippi.'

Balum accepted the drink and let a touch of it run over his tongue. He immediately suppressed a gag to spit it back out. A brackish film of foulness coated his mouth. He set the glass down and elected to remain silent.

'You like single malt?' Carly poured out something resembling a dehydrated man's piss and urged Balum to savor it. 'I've been selling this to all the big guys. You ever go to the Silver Nest? Mung's Gambling House? They love me there. Just mention my name, they'll serve you free drinks all night.'

'What do you think, Balum?' said Aston. 'Worth adding to my collection?'

'Interesting flavor,' was all Balum could muster.

'Indeed,' agreed Aston.

Shane Carly beamed, taking the exchange as a compliment. 'Girls at the Baltimore Club are practically throwing themselves at me when I come in,' he boasted, his pudgy cheeks glowing under miniature marble eyes. 'Everyone wants their hands on this. They practically line up when I travel through Denver.'

Balum returned the glass and kept his mouth shut. The whiskey distributor was either a liar or an imbecile, and more than likely both. As though reading Balum's thoughts, Aston Sanderson abruptly ended the tasting by escorting Shane Carly out the front door with a promise to consider a purchase at some later yet unspecified point in time. When the door was shut behind him Aston returned to the parlor.

'Tell me your opinion of the whiskey.'

'It's foul,' said Balum. 'And the salesman either thinks he can pass off rotgut for good whiskey or he doesn't know the difference between the two.'

Aston nodded in approval. 'Good. If you'd said any differently I'd have sent you out the door after him. Any man who drinks Shane Carly's whiskey is not a man fit to court my daughter. And that's what you're here for, is it not?'

'It is,' replied Balum. 'She's an admirable woman and I aim to treat her accordingly. With your permission I'd like to show her Denver and spend time in her company.'

'Plenty has been said about you. You've become quite famous over the last week.'

'For the wrong reasons. Nelson seems to have found

himself a sleek lawyer.'

'Yes,' mused Aston. 'I've heard other things. They say you made your fortune in the cattle business. Tell me about that.'

'Hard work and luck. That's what it was. We rounded them up in Mexico and drove them to Cheyenne. No input but our own sweat, and with the price high in Cheyenne we made a fine profit.'

The finer details, Ned Witney, the shootouts, the commotion surrounding it, he made no mention of.

'Is that so? How much did you make exactly?'

The question gave Balum an uneasy sensation. The man was out of line.

'I prefer to keep my financial affairs private.'

'I'll not have a bum cavorting about with my daughter,' Aston's voice came back sharply. 'Every nincompoop with a penny to his name has his eye on Sara. That nitwit Irishman peddling whiskey distilled in a privy hole would take her out if he had his druthers. So answer me straight. I need to know you're a man of means. What did you make off that sale?'

Balum held the man's eyes for a moment, a silent struggle between two bulls. He didn't like Aston Sanderson, that much he knew. A prying man he was, built too much in the likeness of Frederick Nelson. Yet the cards had been laid and Aston was the man dealing.

'I made ten thousand,' said Balum. 'And I earned every cent of it.'

Aston's expression took on a faraway look. He brought

a hand to his chin and touched it absentmindedly.

'That's fine indeed,' he said. His eyes drifted to the side, looking at nothing in the room, but seeing something of great interest in his own mind. He looked back at Balum and seemed to regain his toughened composure. 'Very well. You've my permission. I'll expect her back at a decent hour. When do you plan on calling?'

'Tomorrow evening.'

'We'll be expecting you. Now if you'll excuse me, I've matters to attend to.'

He escorted Balum out of the parlor and through the sitting room and, as if he were throwing out Shane Carly, had the door closed before Balum had taken two steps past the frame.

# 11

Balum soon forgot about Aston Sanderson. Not that he didn't see him; he saw him every night, for like clockwork he arrived at the Sanderson residence at five thirty, greeted her parents with a prepared salutation, and took Sara Sanderson away, her arm in his. To the finest restaurants, the theatre, walks in the public park where vendors came in the evenings to sell sweets to children and roses to lovers. To the Silver Nest, the Berlamont Hotel Restaurant, and to the jewelers, where he spent a cowpoke's monthly wages in the space of four days.

Blindness and deafness shrouded him throughout the rest of the day. In the courtroom he had only a mind for the young lady flirting across the aisle. As for Saul Farro and Frederick Nelson, each content with the path the proceedings were taking, he simply stopped noticing them. Johnny Freed's pompous mug, held in a challenging pose in back of the courthouse, went ignored. His friends sought him out, but to catch him was like trapping the wind in a jar. He had time only for Sara Sanderson.

At only one point in the length of five days was his mind torn away from his enchantress. He sat in the courthouse, stealing glances at her and daydreaming of taking her to the far end of the park that night, where darkness would cover their kisses as he held her in his arms. A nudge from an elbow took him out of his reverie.

'They're calling you,' said a voice.

His surroundings came into focus and he sat confused for a moment, then stood and walked the aisle between the prosecutor and defense tables and to the witness stand. With his hand over the bible he swore to tell the truth and was seated.

The District Attorney's questions posed no problem. They had rehearsed what would be asked, and Balum's responses came easy and natural. When he had answered the last of them the attorney returned to his bench and Douglas Crenshaw took the floor. He looked at Balum a moment then turned to the jury and bent his head.

'Balum,' he began. 'A name until recently not too many folks around here had heard of. And a man without a past has little to rest his word on. Is your word good, Mr. Balum?'

'It is.'

'You says it is,' Crenshaw spoke to the jury, 'but what proof do we have? The only word we have that we can scrutinize upon is the deposition you gave to Johnny Freed, U.S. Marshal. Allow me to read a section.'

From the bench he drew the deposition and read aloud two passages.

"Leigha Atkisson shot Saul Farro at the edge of a crevice, which measured a hundred yards deep. He fell into it and died." Crenshaw returned the paper to the bench and made a show of scanning the audience. 'Mr. Balum, answer this. Is that not Mr. Saul Farro seated in the second row of the court, alive and well before our very eyes and before the Lord God?'

'I didn't expect he would have survived that fall…'

'Answer the question, sir,' Crenshaw interrupted. 'Is that the same Saul Farro you claimed under oath was dead?'

'Yes,' Balum said curtly.

'Gentlemen of the jury, the man's word has been proven false. A man who will lie under oath once will lie again.'

'I was wrong, but that…'

'Who exactly is this man?' Crenshaw shouted, cutting Balum's defense off. 'Who are you, Balum? Are you a criminal?'

'No, of course not.'

'You've not been imprisoned before?'

Balum started to respond, but the memory of Bette's Creek rose up, and another, darker memory buried deep in his past.

'Does the name Bette's Creek bring up anything?'

Balum sat silently, teeth clenched together.

'Were you not imprisoned for some time there?'

'By a crooked sheriff who was hanged by the neck, yes.'

'And Mexico. The Belén Jail. Did you not serve time there as well?'

The blood ran from Balum's face and he sat in a cold sweat, staring at the mass of onlookers gathered in the courthouse hall. A crushing sound beat against his eardrums like a surge of waves flung in violent lashings against the rocks

'Well, Balum?'

'For a crime I did not commit, yes.' The words came out softly. He heard them leave his lips like sounds spoken by someone else, somewhere far away.

A flutter of whispers rose over the hall.

'The man has served time in two prisons,' ranted Crenshaw, 'and has clearly lied under oath. Is this the word of a man you will use to pass judgement on my client, Frederick Nelson? I have no further questions, your Honor.'

Chester stood amongst the crowd outside the courthouse. When he spotted Balum exit through the doors with his head down he drew up alongside him and the two walked several blocks in silence before Chester spoke.

'I was inside. Saw what happened. That Crenshaw fellow sure has put his nose up your past. Aside from me, there ain't too many folks around who know about Bette's Creek. He did some digging.'

Balum said nothing. His eyes looked a few feet ahead into the street and his feet took him forward in determined paces.

'I'd always wondered,' said Chester, 'if you was the same Balum in those stories about that Mexican jail. I figured either the stories were just stories, or you would have been too young.' He swung his head over to Balum but found no response there. 'You don't have to say nothing. I won't say nothing either. Let's get us a whiskey.'

In the Berlamont Hotel Restaurant they sat and ordered two whiskeys. Balum had not spoken. The whiskeys arrived and Chester took a strong gulp while Balum only turned his in circles on the table.

'What do you make of the judge giving a week long recess?' Chester attempted a line of conversation. 'How can there be that many cases to go through? Bunch of troublemakers in this town I guess. But it don't matter. Getting you out of that courtroom for a while will do you some good. The Silver Nest has another tournament on the calendar. What do you say you throw your hat in? Take your mind off things awhile.'

Balum took his eyes off the glass. 'I'm riding to Cheyenne. Will's getting married. I wouldn't miss it.'

'Ah, that's good. That's good. Get your head some fresh air. You need to get away from things here, get away from the court, Freed, that girl…'

'She's coming with me.'

'Coming with you?'

'Her parents as well. We leave tomorrow. Her folks will drive a wagon.'

'Jesus, Balum.'

Balum smiled. The melancholy left his face and his

eyes took on the old glimmer. Chester cringed. He looked about the restaurant and leaned forward.

'I see how happy you are about that, Balum. But I'm your friend and I need to speak my mind. You've been spending every free hour with that girl. You're head over heels, and it ain't love, it's infatuation. There's a difference.'

Balum scowled and started to speak but Chester raised a hand.

'Hear me out, Balum. You're under a lot of pressure with the trial, and this girl takes your mind from it. All you can think about is getting married and settling down. You're jumping at the bit. So eager to find what you want you can't see what everybody else does.'

'What do they see?'

'Problems.'

'Name one.'

Chester swung his head in a scan over the restaurant. He leaned on his elbows over the table, the fingers of his hands spread wide. 'What business has Sanderson got going to the jail?'

'Aston?'

'Twice now.'

'Ross hasn't said anything about that.'

'Why would he. Plenty on his plate too, and he ain't a man to gossip.'

'Could be any number of reasons.'

'Balum, take the advice of an old man. I've been where you are now, and I've ignored plenty of advice I should have heeded. I'm telling you there's something ain't right going on and you're barreling forward like you've got blinders on.'

Balum stood and plucked his hat off the table.

'I need to catch some shut eye, Chester. I leave early tomorrow. Good luck at the Silver Nest.'

Chester watched his friend turn and leave through the dining hall doors. He'd upset him, that much was clear. He wondered what opinion Randolph might hold. While he considered this he reached over the table to Balum's untouched glass and tossed its contents down his throat.

# 12

From the hawk's view ten thousand feet above them their figures were but shapeless blemishes on an open and endless plain. The covered carriage the Sandersons drove was short and light and the horses pulling it leaned like browbeaten vassals into the traces. Balum's roan walked in front, side by side with Sara's paint. Massive upthrust peaks of mountaintops loomed unmoving to the west. For hours they rode without a change in the range of craggy summits that towered like lifeless gods on watch over the sprawl of land cast eastward. Under their dominion rode the travelers, all four silent as though carrying out an order to which no refusal could be made. Like four mourners spent by grief, haggard and plodding forward in mindless resolution.

They stopped not for lunch but instead rode through the day while the sun's light cast shadows that slowly shrank and inverted from west to east and stretched out again as the sun retreated and the silhouettes of the horses lengthened into spindly legs of spiders crossing the darkening plains in a garish march.

At night they camped at the base of a cutbank where

pines had taken root and flourished. Dead boughs sat crooked and bent on the ground, and over his knee Balum broke them and made a fire, and they ate in silence and retired to their bedding.

For why such an uneasy atmosphere clouded their journey, Balum blamed a swath of perpetrators. The trial, Nelson, Farro, Freed, even Chester and his unwelcomed warnings which found no fair hearing in Balum's mind.

In the morning they breakfasted in comparable silence. Mrs. Sanderson drank coffee with her face long and set harshly along its formerly beautiful lines. Doubt snuck into Balum. Perhaps he had been too exuberant in inviting Sara to the wedding. It required the accompaniment of her parents; a journey upon which they had no desire to commence. He felt the Sandersons were carrying out the responsibilities of a job. What job, he did not know. Only that its finality was worth the cost of its labor.

Late into the night they arrived in Cheyenne. Two days of fifty mile treks had sapped the travelers, and their legs took them through the Rosemonte Hotel doors like somnambulistic creatures trapped in bodies foreign and uncooperative. The Sandersons disappeared straight to their room. Balum returned to the street and drove the carriage and horses to the livery where they were unhitched and unsaddled, groomed and watered and fed.

When the chores were completed he returned to the Rosemonte and stretched his tired frame over the mattress. Wearily he waited for sleep. It came, in time, but not before an interminable stretch of guilt in which his mind obsessed not over the woman in the room next to him, but on the one inhabiting the room over a brothel floor several blocks away. A room in which he had slept and laughed and made love. A room in which he had whispered her name softly, a name spelled out in flowing black letters across the envelope laying unopened and unread atop his desk in Denver.

Tables covered the front yard of the CW Ranch, each punctuated with a centerpiece of cut flowers. Will wore a tailored broadcloth suit and his young bride walked with a veil dragging twenty feet behind her and smiling with glowing red cheeks all the while.

When the ceremony concluded and the new couple was presented to the public, a feast was offered. Roasted beef, goat, pies, cakes. Liquor was distributed in such quantities that no soul who felt a thirst rise up in him went unsated. A fiddler took up his instrument and set the merry crowd to dancing. Children ran between the tables and screamed and laughed while their parents stuffed their gullets with food and drink.

As the commotion grew, Charles found Balum and took him aside.

'Word of the trial has made its way up,' he said. 'Is it as bad as they're saying?'

'Depends what they're saying.'

'That Nelson's got some crack shot lawyer turning everything around and pinning it on you.'

'He's trying.'

'I heard his brother hired him just for the job.'

Balum flinched. 'What brother?'

'Half-brother, I guess. I don't know. Those are the rumors. Tell me what the story is behind this girl you've brought up. She's pretty. I'll tell you that right now.'

'Sara Sanderson. We met not long ago, but she wants what I want.'

'From where your eyes keep drifting to, I'd be of a mind to disagree.'

'How's that?'

'Come on now, Balum. You've been staring at Angelique ever since you showed up. You just looked at her now!'

Balum looked her way again then pulled his head around, fighting himself.

'And she's been looking at you just as much,' Charles continued. 'So what happened? Up to a few weeks ago she was the gal for you. Now you show up with a new girl on your arm.'

'Angelique doesn't want me, Charles. She said as much before and I didn't listen. I got the point this time.'

'She told you that?'

'In her own way. Look at her now. Here with some fellow.'

'Looks a little old to me,' said Charles.

Balum shrugged.

'Get ready,' Charles said under his breath. 'Here she comes now. I'll leave you to it.'

Charles turned and left Balum standing in the open, a queasiness in his belly that couldn't be blamed on the food. She came walking through the tables with a hand lifting the length of her dress. Her hair shone in immaculate locks, piled atop her head underneath a summer bonnet. The urge came over him to open his arms, to embrace her tightly against him, hold her there and smell the sweet scent of her neck uncovered. Instead he held his arms rigid against his body.

'Balum,' she said when she was close. Her head tilted slightly, and though warmth showed through her eyes, it was mixed with confusion and a hesitation much unlike her.

'Angelique,' he replied with a nod of his head.

'I'm so glad you came,' she said. 'Did you get my letter? I've been trying to reach you.'

He stumbled over what to say. Before he had formed a reply, Sara's voice appeared next to him.

'Balum! Come dance with me.'

She took him by the arm without a word of greeting directed at Angelique and pulled him away to the matted down grass in front of the fiddler where couples clapped their hands and bounced on a rhythm of celebration.

He looked back, once. She stood watching him, alone, her dress held in her hands. Not a look of anger on her face, or irritation or disdain. A look altogether different. One he knew he was the cause of and, though he wished it, had no solution for the cure.

Before the celebration had come to a close they left. A goodbye to Charles, to Will and Tessa. Balum's eyes searched for Angelique, though for what purpose he wasn't sure. He wanted to see her, hug her, explain things. Something. But she was gone, and Sara's parents had already started the wagon homeward.

The sound of music faded behind them. The notes grew fainter and disappeared out over the grandeur of the plains stretching endlessly southward. The roan and the paint rode alongside the carriage. They stopped late in the evening and rose early the next day as though no time had passed at all.

Under a red morning sun they lumbered forward. The wagon wheels creaked in metronomed rhythm. Balum searched for his tobacco but he was out. He wiped the sweat from his brow and watched his mind skip like a kaleidoscope through his current burdens. He fought for something enjoyable on which to dwell but the trial would seep back into his mind, Nelson with it, Saul Farro lurking and waiting in Denver.

When Sara pulled up alongside Balum and smiled, he gazed foolishly at her beauty as though a nubile young pixie had been sent to rescue him from his demons.

'That was a beautiful wedding,' she said with her eyes wide and searching.

'It was.'

'I loved Tessa's dress. I want mine to be like that.'

'It was nice.'

'And I want music at my wedding. Fiddlers and lots of food and table settings like they had,' she searched Balum's face. 'Are you going to marry me, Balum, or are you just enjoying your time?'

Balum's breath caught. She was a forward girl, yet even for her the question was overtly brazen. It caught him unprepared.

'I want to settle down and have a ranch with a wife and children,' he admitted.

'Oh, so do I,' she quickly agreed. 'Think of what we could have together. Think of what we could do when we combine what we have.'

Balum rode with his eyes plastered over a near featureless landscape.

'With what you and I have between us,' she went on, 'we could find the perfect ranch. Buy the most beautiful spot of land, hire the best builders in all of Denver. I'll start the search as soon as we get back.'

He consented with a nod of his head, though his eyes did not stray from the bleakness that distended out from his horse's ears as far as his vision would take him.

# 13

Another day in court. Enough to lose count of them. As he stood in front of the mirror of the hotel room in the early light of dawn he wished only to know the number left. May he move on with his life, he thought. A life with Sara Sanderson, a house in the countryside, mornings spent together on a rocker on the porch. The more he thought about it the more the fantasy grew in his head. He projected onto it all the joy his mind would muster.

He pulled on his boots and placed his hat over his head. Every movement was carried out in a way that spared his eyes having to land on the letter still resting on his desk. He walked wide of it on the way out the door and left the Berlamont Hotel by way of the front door where Daniel Randolph surprised him in the street.

'Morning there, early riser,' Randolph tipped his hat. 'I thought I'd invite you to breakfast. No good sitting in court on an empty stomach.'

'Let's see if we can fill it.'

They took seats in the cafe across from the Denver Commercial Bank and ordered eggs and grits and bacon and endless cups of coffee brewed black and scalding.

Their tongues balked at the bitterness but they drank it anyway while Randolph filled Balum in on Chester's continued streak of luck at the Silver Nest. They ate breakfast and rambled on to each other on a field of meaningless topics until the hour came for Balum to leave for the courthouse. He made to rise from the table but Randolph stuck out a hand and motioned for Balum to wait.

'There's something else,' he said. 'Something I saw last night and thought I should tell you.'

'Alright. Let's hear it.'

'I hit a bad streak of luck at the Silver Nest last night. Lost some money I shouldn't have gambled. When I left I took a walk, ruminating mostly and kicking myself. Didn't feel like going back home. I didn't pay much attention to where I was going, and I ended up on High Street, just as you were riding in with the Sandersons. It was late. I was in a foul mood and you looked pretty haggard yourself, so I stayed on the other side of the street and didn't say anything. I saw you climb up onto that carriage seat and drive it away with the two horses trailing after you. When I got to the end of that street I figured it was no use beating myself up anymore and I'd be better off asleep in bed. So I turned around and came walking right back down High Street. Past the Sanderson's house.'

'What are you getting at?'

'They had a visitor.'

'Alright.'

'Saul Farro.'

Balum's shoulders tightened and he bent his head forward. 'What do you mean Saul Farro?'

'He walked right out the front door. Shook Aston Sanderson's hand before he left.'

Balum snorted and looked away. Randolph waited for a reply, but none came.

'You know any reason why Farro would be dropping in on the Sandersons late in the evening? Or any time at all, for that matter?'

'Couldn't have been him,' said Balum.

'It was.'

'No. It was well past sunset. Dark out. It could have been anyone.'

'Balum, you know full well there's no mistaking Saul Farro. He's near six and a half feet tall and built like a buffalo.'

Balum was still shaking his head, his eyes not wanting to meet his friend.

'Things don't add up, Balum. You've been spending every free hour with the Sanderson girl while that trial is getting away from you.'

'Don't bring the girl into this.'

'I will, because you're my friend. And somebody's got to tell you.'

'You and Chester both.'

'She's bad news, Balum. Her and her family are mixed up in this somehow. You're not seeing what everybody else is.'

Balum stood abruptly and glanced out the window.

'I've got to be going. Trial's about to start.'

'Balum,' said Randolph, but the man was already gone and out the door.

Balum crossed the street, dodging wagons and narrowly beating a small cadre of goats being herded down the dusty avenue by two sorry looking ranchers on the backs of skeleton horses. He walked with his head bent forward as if fighting a gale of wind.

Daniel Randolph couldn't have been right. He'd been gambling, most likely drinking, and it was dark out. Why everyone was so set against Sara he couldn't figure. She was a beauty. Was it jealousy? Doubtful. Neither Chester nor Randolph were the jealous type. Just overly cautious perhaps.

As though his thoughts brought her apparition to life, Sara Sanderson waved to him from the next block. Damn beautiful, he thought. Her cheeks were flushed and her eyes glowing, a seductive smile playing across her face. He took her in his arms and pressed her body against his, feeling her breasts against his chest, her small waist. She giggled and kissed him on the cheek. He wanted to take her right there, throw her over his shoulder and carry her to the hotel where he would toss her to the bed and crawl on top of her, rip the dress from her tender body and press himself into her, lose himself inside her.

'My,' she giggled, 'you're awfully excited to see me.'

'I am. You're the only thing that relieves the stress I'm under.'

'Aw, you poor thing,' she brought a gloved hand to his

face and drew her fingers along his jaw. 'It'll be over soon. And when it is we'll have all the time in the world, just to ourselves. By the way, I talked to the manager at the bank this morning. The Denver Commercial. In order to begin surveying land and placing bids, our names will have to be joined together on the same account.'

'The same account?'

'It's just a formality, dear. We can go in this afternoon and complete the paperwork.' She drew close to him again and wrapped her arms around him. He could feel her breasts against his chest as she brought her mouth close to his ear. 'We'll be so happy together, my love. Now let's get you to the courthouse.'

They entered through the double doors together and took seats on opposite side of the aisle. Ross Buckling was again present. Balum eased down next to him and they shook hands.

'Couldn't stay away, eh Ross?'

'Things are getting interesting. Freed told me yesterday he's expected to take the stand today.'

Balum only folded his hands across his lap and waited. Across the aisle he could feel Saul Farro's eyes searching him out. He thought back to Randolph's warning and wondered again if there was any truth to it. His mind turned it over. He found it hard to concentrate. Sara's notion of adding her name to his bank account troubled him, though he denied it to himself.

Judge Vanderloop entered the hall and Balum's mind let itself fall into the mechanical proceedings of the trial.

115

The first witness to be called was not Johnny Freed, but the name of a public notary whom Balum did not know.

The man rose from the back and shuffled forward to the witness stand. He sat hunched and small looking, and when questioned he would squirm as if being forced onto a bronc he'd rather not ride.

'You've seen plenty of penmanship in your line of work, this is true?' said Douglas Crenshaw.

'I have,' squirmed the notary.

'Have you ever come across samples of the writing claimed to belong to Jonathan Atkisson, Jeb Darrow, and this half-breed named Joe?'

Balum cringed in his seat at Crenshaw's description of Joe.

'I haven't,' said the notary.

'So there is no evidence to support that the three affidavits Mr. Balum has turned over were actually written by those men?'

'Well, their signatures, I guess.'

'Have you any samples of the men's' signatures?'

'No.'

'Is it possible they might have been forged?'

The notary shifted in his chair. 'Possible, I guess.'

'That's all your honor.'

The notary returned to the back of the hall with his eyes on his feet as he walked. Ross and Balum exchanged glances and the next witness was called to the stand; U.S. Marshal Johnny Freed.

He raised his hand high in the air and shot his eyes

over to Balum as he swore to tell the whole truth and nothing but. In the witness stand he sat straight and important looking, a different demeanor altogether than that of the notary. His chin tilted up and his nose seemed to pinch tight in the center of his narrow face.

'Mr. Freed,' said Crenshaw. 'Where were you when Balum brought in Mr. Nelson?'

'At the jail, sir.'

'Can you describe to me the state of the prisoner when he was turned over?'

'I can,' announced Freed in his loud pinched voice. 'He'd been abused. Treated unfairly, nearly tortured. He'd been starved, kept from water, and tied over a saddle for so long that his skin was rubbed raw from his neck to his belly. He hadn't been allowed to relieve himself and you could see the damage that did to him.'

At this point the District Attorney objected. 'What does this have to do with the case at hand, your Honor?'

'It has everything to do with the case,' said Crenshaw before the judge could respond. 'What this treatment shows is a hatred toward my client on part of the man who brought him in.'

'Overruled,' the judge said from his seat.

'Did Balum have any reason as to why he treated the defendant so viciously?' asked Crenshaw.

'He did not. In fact he seemed to take pride in how badly he'd abused the man.'

'That's all, your Honor,' said Crenshaw.

The District Attorney followed. He put forward a well

thought out barrage of questions to Freed, but the young Marshal was adamant and refused to back down in his assertions. He left the witness stand looking pleased with himself and scowled down on Balum when he passed him like a dominant buck having just bested his closest rival in an antler fight.

The court adjourned. Judge Vanderloop announced that session would open at noon the following day, and the hall emptied. Those previously packed together in the courtroom soon dispersed into the streets of Denver, and Balum found himself disappearing with them. A recklessness boiled up in him. He had an urge to lose himself in drink, in women, in cards, anything that would take his mind form the trial. Sara waited for him somewhere. He couldn't face her now, nor could he explain to himself the reason behind his reluctance. Why did the Baltimore Club call to him? Why the massage parlor? The constant thoughts of Angelique?

He watched himself as though from the air. Himself, the man in the street, tall, broad shouldered, toughened by time and by hardship. Beaten.

Not beaten yet, he told himself. All was not lost. The trial would resume tomorrow; the jury would not let themselves be hoodwinked by such a buffoon as Douglas Crenshaw. He still had Sara. He would be married. A wife, children, a ranch, tranquility. It all awaited him.

The barman in the Mexican cantina set before him a glass of tequila and a bowl of chicharrones.

Balum reached into his pocket to pay but the barman

held up a hand.

'*Cortesía de la casa.*'

Balum accepted, and the barman left without explanation. The first sip stung his throat. It burned, hot and dagger-like in his belly. The feeling of expansion took hold of his head, a lessening of tension. Relief. He took another sip. The darkness of the cantina comforted him. The murmur of Spanish, the smells of freshly made tortillas. He took a chicharrón from the bowl and let the salt mix with the sting of tequila in his mouth.

Out of the darkness a figure rose. A tall man, sombrero in hand. He approached Balum's table and pulled out a chair, then sat and rested the sombrero over his knee.

'*Buenas tardes,*' the man said.

Balum nodded, indifferent. The man sitting across from him, though uninvited, intrigued Balum. He was dressed as a Mexican vaquero, yet physically did not look the part. Too tall, the features of his face wrong. He waited for the man to speak again.

'*Vengo con un consejo,*' he said.

'I haven't asked for any advice,' said Balum.

'*Ya lo sé. Pero se lo voy a dar de toda manera.*'

'*Bueno. Dime.*'

'*Usted se ha metido con mala gente. Gente que le va a llevar a la ruina.*'

'*Qué gente?*'

'*Los que asaltan los trenes.*'

'*Quiénes?*'

119

'*Los Sanderson.*'

Balum leaned back in the chair. He looked hard at the man across the table from him, searching his face, his demeanor. It made no sense.

'You telling me the Sandersons are train robbers?'

'That's exactly what I'm telling you.'

Balum felt his face react to the man's English. It came out perfectly, without accent, and completely unexpected.

'What evidence do you have?' asked Balum.

'Evidence that would put me in a bad light, were I to reveal it to the law.'

'Why are you telling me this? Why help me?'

'I know who you are now. You are the famous Balum, *de La Cárcel de Belén.* Everyone here knows that now. Many owe you. Who did not have a friend, a father, a son, there in that prison? For me it was my brother. My half-brother, Juventino Costas.

Memories Balum had pushed down for years rose up from the dark crevices of his mind. Tino Costas was among them.

'What's your name?' said Balum.

'Caesar Costas,' he said, then stood and placed the sombrero on his head and paused, looking at Balum across the table. '*Ten cuidado.*'

'Careful of what?'

'*Las cosas que hará uno...por el amor de una mujer.*'

He vanished back into the dim. His companions rose, the sound of spurs and leather chaps infused the darkness, and they left through the door. Balum sat with the empty tequila glass, repeating the man's words in his head.

*The things one will do...for the love of a woman.*

# 14

Sleep brought no consolation. He woke in a state of agitation no less draining than the day before. The sources of his vexation were too numerous to know which to concentrate on first.

Sara wanted her name on his bank account. Chester claimed Aston was visiting the jail house, Randolph insisted he saw Saul Farro at the Sanderson residence. The trial was turning on its head. Nelson appeared more innocent every day. The message from Caesar Costas in the cantina last night appeared so preposterous he hardly knew what to think of it.

And the letter.

It sat on the desk, untouched, lurking behind every thought that floated across Balum's conscience. He leapt from the bed suddenly and snatched it up, then paused, looking at the lettering on the envelope. He replaced it, dressed himself, and took it up again. The trial was not scheduled to begin until noon. He would take a ride. A long ride, out to the foothills, where he could be alone. To sit with a problem, a plug of tobacco in his cheek, with time to study the tangle of woes besetting him; that was what he needed.

He tucked the envelope into his shirt pocket and left his room.

The stares from the townspeople were losing their shock. They followed him out the hotel and down the boardwalks; sideways glances and brief flashes of eyelids stealing peeks as he crossed to the edge of town and past the corral and through the livery doors.

The liveryman's apprentice, a boy in overalls who should have been at school, walked the length of the stalls scooping grain into the feeding buckets hanging on the gate doors.

'The old timer ain't in,' said the boy when Balum came through the livery doors. 'He's done caught ill.'

'That's alright. I'm taking the roan out for a ride.'

'I'd help you get him saddled but I've got to be off to the feed store.'

'You run along,' said Balum. 'I'll saddle him up and be back in the afternoon.'

'There's some apples past their day in that barrow yonder,' the boy motioned to the end of the livery where bales of hay were stacked a dozen feet into the air. 'Your roan's got a taste for 'em. I got to be going now. Good luck with the trial, Mr. Balum.'

Balum's boots fell silently on the dust of the livery floor after the boy had left. Horses watched him walk the length of the building with their oblong heads protruding out from their stall gates, their great jaws masticating, eyes leveled solid at the stranger. The roan waited in the end stall. He shook his head at Balum's approach.

The wheelbarrow mentioned by the boy was indeed filled with apples past their prime, rotten and dimpled, flies buzzing in senseless circles over the mass of piled fruit. He took one in his hand and held it out over the gate. The roan curled its lips back and snatched it up as though it were a trick taught and practiced a hundred times over. Balum treated it to another, then waited for the roan to return to the grain.

He watched his horse, enjoying the silence of the livery until it was broken by Sara Sanderson's voice at the livery doors.

'There you are,' she exclaimed. 'I've been looking all over for you dear. What on earth are you doing in the livery?'

'I thought I'd take a ride. The city's got me feeling like a bull in a bucking chute.'

'We were supposed to meet after court yesterday. The bank manager was expecting us. I feel rather foolish now. I prefer to keep my appointments.'

'Ah, yes,' he mumbled. He stood beside the stall at the edge of the piled bales of hay, out of the walkway between the two rows of horses. Sara walked towards him, the two lines of horses observing the newcomer in the same way they had followed Balum. He watched her, his eyes unable to avoid the sight of her body wrapped in a thin dress, the neckline creeping down just enough to give a hint of what might lay below. She gave an extra wiggle to her hips, aware of his eyes on her.

'This is important, Balum,' she said, turning the corner of the roan's stall and stopping inches in front of him. Her hands reached out and touched his waistline. 'Don't you want to find a place together?'

'Yes, of course.'

'Then you need to add me to your account. It's how these things are done.'

Her hands moved up his chest, slowly curving over to where his neck met his shoulders.

'I just thought…'

'Oh you poor thing,' she cooed. 'You're so tense. This trial has you so stressed.'

She drew closer. The tip of her cleavage rose and fell on her breath, inches below his face. Her body touched his; her thighs against him, her forearms on his chest, her breasts pressed into him. She dug her fingers gently into his neck and shoulders and looked into his eyes.

Balum's hands found her waist and he bent and kissed her. Her mouth opened immediately, inviting him in, and her tongue slid over his. Balum felt his cock engorge and rise in his trousers. It pressed into her, gently into her belly.

'Oh,' she brought a hand to her lips as if something indiscreet had happened and stepped back slightly. The fingers of her hand traced a line down his torso and twisted and cupped the throbbing mass of his crotch. 'So this is where all your stress is. You poor thing. That trial is so nasty. Let me help you. Then we'll go to the bank and get this all sorted out.'

Deftly, she unbuttoned his trousers and reached her

hand inside while at the same time returning her mouth to his, her lips full and wet, softly pressing into his. Her hand grabbed his exposed shaft and began to stroke the length of it, slowly, her fingers applying pressure. She took one of his hands in hers and brought it to her breast, turning herself over to him.

Balum felt his thoughts vanish. Urgency replaced them. A driving passion, a buildup of weeks of longing. He popped open the buttons running down the front of her dress and gripped her bare breasts in his hand, squeezing them, bending to suck on the nipples while she tugged at his cock. She knelt suddenly and set her knees in the hay. His cock waved just above her upturned face.

'Will this make you feel better, honey?' she asked.

Balum nodded and placed his hand at the back of her head and slid his manhood into her open mouth. She took it, her eyes never leaving his. The sound of moaning, slurping, whimpering, rose up from the livery floor. Her mouth came off his cock and her tongue came out to trace its contours, lick the tip, the shaft, tickle his hanging balls. She pressed his wet dick against her cheek and looked into his eyes.

'We're going to be so happy together, dear,' she whispered while the saliva-covered shaft wetted her cheek. 'I'm going to take all that stress from you. Then we'll go to the bank and get all this business sorted out.'

He scarcely heard her. He drew his hips back and plunged his cock back into her mouth, thrusting into the warmth and wetness and losing himself in her moans. She pushed him away suddenly and stood, turned around, and lifted her dress over her hips. Underneath she wore nothing; no bloomers, no undergarments, no leggings. With her hamstrings straight, she bent forward at the waist and touched her hands to the ground in front of her. Her firm round ass rose up towards him, the cheeks spread apart to reveal her pink asshole and the delicate lips of her pussy, glistening with wetness and waiting to be filled.

He took hold of her by the hips and felt his cock slide along her wet vagina, slipping against the warmth of her thighs, until he pressed its tip against the hot tightness of her pussy and thrust himself into her. She gasped out and he rammed his shaft hard and deep into her. The smack of his thighs against the back of hers clapped out in the open livery. His fingers pressed into the firm flesh of her hips, sinking slightly into the skin.

She moaned out as he pounded her from behind. Neither cared of the consequences; they both needed this, each for their own reasons. She reached behind him and cupped his balls in her hand. When she felt them tighten, when his hands clenched ferociously onto her hips, she pulled away from him suddenly. Dropping to her knees she spun around suddenly and took his shaft again in her hand and rose her face to meet his eyes.

'You like that, baby?' her voice came in a whine.

'Yes,' he gasped.

'You want it back in my mouth?'

'Yes,' he uttered again, his vision hazy.

'You'll take me to the bank?'

'Yes,' he said, mechanically, desperately.

She sunk the shaft past her lips and along her tongue, and let him rock his hips back and forth until his cock erupted in a stream of cum, shooting hot and thick into the back of her throat.

She did not let him go. Her mouth tightened. With one hand at his back, the other took the base of his cock and gave short strokes, squeezing the last of his cum into her mouth as he groaned in pleasure above her. When he drew it from her mouth a string of cum clung to her lip. She reached a finger out and lifted it, then sucked it back into her mouth and swallowed.

'You feel better, baby?' she asked.

Balum's legs shook slightly. A response was too much to muster. His eyes closed and his head floated upward, and suddenly, nothing seemed to matter.

# 15

Not until shortly after noon, as the court proceedings got underway, did Balum begin to regain focus.

He had not taken the ride as planned. The envelope still sat unopened in his shirt pocket. Instead he had accompanied Sara Sanderson to the Denver Commercial Bank, where they had sat together before the bank manager's quizzical looks and signed the required paperwork which transferred Sara's name onto his account, authorizing full access over its funds.

Seated in the densely packed courthouse, the nearly tactile sense of excitement brought Balum's mind to a focal point. The trial was nearly over. Only two witnesses were left. At the end of their testimonies the jury would retire to the jury room to hash out a verdict on the fate of Frederick Nelson. Balum could feel his breath come quickly. His hands felt clammy. He looked across the aisle for Sara but his eyes found only her parents seated together, eyes straight ahead. He swung his head to where their focus was directed and saw Saul Farro turned sideways in his seat with his head crooked around facing the back.

Balum cocked his head. Had there been a look

exchanged just then? No, he told himself. He was imagining things.

The time for doubt was broken by Judge Vanderloop's entrance into the courtroom. In short order, Douglas Crenshaw called Saul Farro to the stand. The enormous man's frame took up the seat as no other witness had. He sat with his torso leaned forward in a challenge directed at the entire hall.

'Mr. Saul Farro,' began Crenshaw. 'Can you tell us what your relationship was to the Oregon Expedition, and to my client, Frederick Nelson?'

'I can. Nelson hired me and my brother as guides.'

'Do you dispute any of the assertions made by Mr. Balum concerning Mr. Nelson?'

'All of 'em!' shouted Saul. 'Every single one.'

'Tell the court please, just what happened on that expedition.'

'Everything started just fine. Then that Balum fellow, he starts to get a craw up his ass.'

'Watch your language,' interjected the judge.

'Anyway,' continued Saul, 'he gets to drinking. Fighting. Turns out he's a regular drunk. A troublemaker. Chasing after the women, scaring folks. He picked a fight with my brother Gus and me. Got so bad we had to throw him and his Injun buddy off the expedition. Well, he didn't like that much so he come huntin' us. Killed my brother. Shot him dead. Him and his buddy, they killed a poor young boy goes by the name of Billy Gunter. They shot a war hero as well, Major Shroud. Balum tried to kill me, tried to kill Nelson. He's a maniac. A killer through and through. Them folks on the Oregon Expedition were lucky to get away. Nelson; he wasn't. Balum caught him, tied him up, decided to bring him into Denver with this cockamamie story that's all nothing but a bunch of goddamn horse shit anyway.'

'Farro!' shouted the judge. 'I won't warn you again.'

'Is everything you've told us here the truth, Mr Farro?' asked Crenshaw.

'You bet it is.'

'Thank you.'

The District Attorney rose and set into Farro with questions meant to pick his story apart. He pried at the edges, looking for cracks, seeking more information which might throw doubt on what had been said. But Saul, though a brute, was no fool. He stuck to his story. As though he had been coached on how to react to the questioning, he kept his answers to a minimum, often only a word or two, and offered no further details other than what was specifically asked. The cross-examination lasted nearly half an hour. When the District Attorney returned to his seat he did so in a manner of abjection, his head low and his brow furrowed in defeat.

Without any pause, Saul Farro took his seat and Frederick Nelson was called to the stand. Crenshaw paced in front of the jurors.

'Mr Nelson,' he began. 'How are you today?'

'Still sore, sir. I was treated mighty rough on the way here.'

'Mr Nelson, we have heard Saul Farro's testimony. Anything you would disagree with there?'

'Saul Farro is an upstanding citizen. A solid man. Every word he spoke was God's own truth.'

'Is there anything you would like to add? What reason would Balum have for treating you so harshly? For making up all these lies?'

'I'll tell you why. Just like Saul said, he was chasing the women. But he's a rotten man, and they could see through him. He had his eyes set on Leigha Atkisson, Jonathan Atkisson's daughter. She was in love with me however, and this vexed him. When she wouldn't degrade herself by giving him her company, he took his vengeance out on me.'

Nelson bent his head and put a hand to his eyes. From where Balum sat he could see the man's shoulders shudder. When Nelson raised his head again a tear was at his eye.

'I'll be damned,' mumbled Balum.

'He crying?' whispered Ross Buckling next to him.

'We could have had a beautiful life together,' Nelson confessed to the courtroom. 'We were in love. But sometimes evil lurks in the shadows. Hatred and vileness. That's my story. Balum couldn't have the woman he desired, so he decided no man should have her. He killed nearly all my men, save for Saul, and tied me up, mistreated me, and hoped to have me hanged by the neck until dead, and all for spite.'

A commotion rose up in the courtroom. Judge Vanderloop brought the gavel down several times over and shouted for silence, but Nelson's testimony was too rich.

From the back a voice shouted over the din, 'Hang that murderer Balum!'

The judge beat the gavel over the sound block and shouted until the hall returned to calm.

'If you people can't sit quiet I'll have you all leave and we'll carry the rest of this trial out in private. Got that? Now quiet down.'

But the commotion was over. The news was out. Crenshaw retired to his bench and the District Attorney rose to question the defendant in as unproductive a manner as he had Saul Farro. He asked for proof of the purported romance but Nelson eloquently responded that his heart was proof enough. He was unbreakable. A well-spoken man, good looking and confident, Nelson found the jury and those in attendance sobbing with him, captivated by his story of lost love and the cruel vengefulness of his rival.

When he finally stepped down from the stand there were no more witnesses to call, no more questions to ask. Closing arguments were made. The District Attorney attempted to remind the jury of the facts of the case. The affidavits, the value of the word of a Deputy Marshal. His implorings fell on stone-faced men sitting tall in the jury box. When Crenshaw took the floor their expressions softened. He spoke with authority, with the voice of a victor. He decried the treatment of his client, reminded the jury of Freed's testimony, the notary, of Balum's history of incarceration, and the sad tale of Nelson's lost love. He finished with a flourish and a bow worthy of the star

133

performer in a Shakespearean opera, and took his seat.

The twelve members of the jury rose and filed out in a single line through the door guarded by a bailiff and ensconced themselves in the jury room. The double doors at the back of the courthouse opened and a waft of fresh air entered. Balum looked across the aisle for Sara, but once again found her absent. He caught Aston's eye, briefly, but the man quickly looked away.

'I need some fresh air,' said Ross Buckling next to him. 'You coming with?'

'No.'

'You just gonna sit there? Might be awhile before they come up with a verdict.'

'Ross,' said Balum. 'Has Aston Sanderson visited Nelson in jail?'

'Couple of times he has. Thought you knew that.'

Balum ran a hand through his hair. He yearned for a plug of tobacco. Something to settle his nerves.

'Come on, Balum. Let's get you out of this courthouse. I ain't gonna let you just sit there. You're liable to fall over dead of worry before that jury's ready. Let's go.'

They rose and left the dark courthouse hall for the sunbaked dust of the Denver streets where they stood side by side, tobacco chewed and savored and spit, while the final bets on Nelson's future were laid in generous odds.

# 16

Through the bailiff-guarded door they came walking. Twelve men, somber-faced and righteous under the weight of duty. Into their seats they filed themselves where they sat facing forward and facing nowhere; twelve men possessing the knowledge of the defendant's fate of which they alone were the deciders.

The overflowing courtroom with its benches crammed and the aisles stuffed with the standing reached a silence deeper than what it could have were it empty. The judge gave the gavel a crack over the sound block. The sound shot through Balum like a .44 bullet. He jerked, then tightened his fingers into his fists and waited.

'Has the jury reached a verdict?' asked the judge of the jury foreman.

'We have, your honor.'

'Mr. Crenshaw, Mr. Nelson. Please rise and face the jury.'

The clanking of Nelson's chains accompanied his movements.

'Mr. Brown,' nodded the judge to the foreman.

'Superior Court of Denver, in the matter of the

People of the United States of America versus Frederick Nelson, case number B three four nine six. We the jury in the above entitled action find the defendant Frederick Nelson not guilty in the crime of murder.'

Balum felt his legs turn light. A fog clouded his eyes and the voice of the foreman gargled into meaninglessness as more legal jargon was recited to the court amongst groans and cheers from the assembled citizenry.

The bailiff took a ring of keys from his belt and unlocked the chains wound tight around Nelson's wrists and ankles. Liberated from his manacles, Nelson rose his fists into the air and turned to the crowd. He shook them over his head and grinned. His eyes met Balum's and held them a moment. Saul Farro squeezed his way down the aisle and the two men clasped their great hands together. Even Johnny Freed managed to reach Nelson through the commotion and extend his hand to the newly-innocent man.

All around them was the air of victory. Crenshaw received slaps on the back and he in turn squeezed the shoulders of his triumphant defendant. The crowd moved like fish crowded into a bucket, squirming past one another, some for the exit, others to find their bookmakers.

Balum searched again for Sara and again found only her absence.

'Let's go, Balum,' said Ross. 'Nothing more to do here.'

The two men edged along the side wall toward the back double doors. At the far end of the court Chester and

Randolph stood waiting. They gave Balum a pat on the back in some small measure of reassurance and the four left together through the open court doors and into the street where they walked quickly away from the hysteria of the masses.

'What'll you do now, Balum?' asked Chester when they'd reach a relatively silent section of street.

Balum let out a long breath with his eyes glazed over.

'Whatever you decide,' said Ross, 'don't go gunning after Nelson. Or Farro for that matter. The law won't look too kindly on it. Not that I wouldn't, but I'm talking about Freed. You hear me, Balum?'

Balum nodded.

'You boys stay out of trouble,' said the Sheriff. He looked at Chester and Daniel. 'Keep him busy. Take him to the Baltimore Club, sit him in a game of poker, anything to keep his mind off it. And keep him off the drink.'

Balum's friends accepted the advice and when Ross had left they turned to him.

'I know you won't be in any mood for the Baltimore Club,' said Daniel. 'Sheriff's right though; you need your mind occupied. How about a game at the Silver Nest? There's another tournament starting up tonight. Still time to get in.'

'I'd lose my money,' said Balum. 'My head's not in it.'

'Come watch then,' said Chester. 'I'll be playing.'

'What the hell,' said Balum. 'Let's go.'

The first floor of the Silver Nest was a mix of emotion. Nearly every man there had bet on the trial, and among the gathered there were none that could not be divided into winners and losers. The latter gave Balum nods and mumbles of encouragement when he entered. The winners paid him little mind.

They crossed the barroom to the stairs where a burly gentleman dressed in finery held his hand up for the entrance fee to the second story.

'Shane Carly says to tell you he sent us,' said Balum.

'Never heard of him,' said the gatekeeper.

'I figured as much.'

'Who's Shane Carly?' asked Chester.

'Nobody, apparently. Just some fool itching to be important.'

They paid the fee and ascended into the more eloquently furnished upper deck. The tables had been prepared and men were beginning to gather as the hour of the tournament approached.

Balum felt sweat bead on his temples. It wouldn't be enough to stand and watch; he knew that much. He longed for a drink. Multiple drinks. Enough to drown his thoughts out and put him to sleep for days at a stretch.

'You ok, Balum?' asked Randolph. They stood at the edge of the room along the balcony overlooking the street.

'I changed my mind. I'm going to throw in on a game.'

'You sure you're in a state to gamble?'

'I sure as hell ain't in a state to stand around watching. What's the buy-in?'

'Fifty dollars. Steep, I know.'

'If I have to lose fifty dollars to calm my mind it'll be worth it. How much time have I got?'

'A good half hour.'

'I'm going to the bank. I'll be right back. Tell the gamesmaster there's another hat in the ring.'

His boots smacked the stairs down to the the main floor where he pushed through the drinkers clear through to the swinging doors and out onto the street. He did not walk blindly; he knew Nelson or Farro walked those same streets. He nearly wished to come upon them, for the fools to say something, start a fight. But they were nowhere, and he reached the bank just before closing time with the sweat still gathering at his brow.

'I'd like to make a withdrawal,' he said to the teller behind the iron bars.

The teller stood mute with his mouth slightly open. 'Balum, right?' he said finally.

'That's right. I've got my account information.'

'Let me get the manager,' said the teller, and turned for the back offices. When he returned the bank manager came with him.

'My employee says you've come to make a withdrawal?' the manager enunciated the simple request as a question.

'That's right.'

'Mr. Balum, your account has already been withdrawn.'

'What do you mean?'

'Ms. Sanderson took out the entire sum in cash this

afternoon. Shortly after you signed her over to your account.'

'What do you mean the entire sum?'

'I mean all of it, Mr. Balum.'

'How much is left?'

The bank manager looked at the teller and then back to Balum. 'There's nothing left. That's what I'm telling you. Your account is empty. She took every last dollar. Down to the cent.'

Balum took a step back and put a hand to the stubble on his jaw. The manager and the teller watched him look slowly around the bank, then turn and leave with his shoulders bent forward and the handle of his Dragoon revolver shining in its holster.

No clear path of logic guided his steps. There was no plan of action he had considered; neither actions nor consequences. Emotion guided him. It took him down Main Street and past the hotels, away from the general stores and barbershop, off the boardwalks shaded under awnings and to the fashionable homes of High Street.

At his knock the blue painted door opened and Aston Sanderson's face greeted him on the other side.

'Balum. Come in,' he gestured. 'I thought I might see you soon.'

'Where is Sara?'

'She's about. Come to the parlor. Have a drink with me.'

Just as before, Shane Carly stood in the parlor pouring whiskey into tumblers lined along a mantel. The splotch-faced man of blubbered physique wrinkled his lips at Balum when he saw him come through the parlor doorway with Aston.

'I'm not in the mood for a drink,' said Balum.

'That's too bad,' said Aston. 'You could use one.'

A rustle sounded behind Balum. Aston's eyes followed it, and Balum turned on his heel. A moment of incomprehension overtook Balum's face.

Frederick Nelson stood before him.

From the parlor doorway came another blur of motion. Balum turned, and with a reflex a half second too late, threw his hands up to protect his face as Saul Farro swung a section of engraved crown moulding that dropped him into a formless heap on the floor.

# 17

The sensation of being dragged over distance woke him. It was night. The outlines of people and objects weaved and shimmered in the darkness. He attempted to gain control of his feet but they were tied. His hands as well; the wrists bound tight with rope. He felt himself be lifted from the ground and he let out an oomph when thrown belly-first over a saddle. The rope trailing from his wrists was looped under the horse's belly and brought around his ankles and cinched tight, causing his frame to curve tightly over the horse in a full-body embrace. With his face resting against the horse's flank his eyes could see the edge of the saddle which he knew to be his. The horse he also knew, for there was no mistaking the roan.

The sound of horses' footfalls striking hardpack rose up in number and the roan was led with them. Turning his head to the side, Balum watched the last buildings grow small as they rode out of Denver. He felt blood slowly gathering in his head low down against the roan's flank. He struggled to move but there was no give to be found in the ropes. He passed out again and fell into a fitful sleep.

He woke again when the horses stopped. Starlight

reflected off the dew covering the grass at the roan's fetlocks. He could hear the rustle of tack; saddles coming off horses, the sound of a brush scraped over coats.

'Saul,' Aston Sanderson's voice carried in the night. 'Untie Balum and take him out where he can relieve himself.'

'Why don't we just leave him right there on the horse?' asked Nelson. 'Let him shit himself. See how it feels.'

'You can treat him as bad as you want when we're done. For now we need him and his horse in working order.'

The rope underneath the roan's belly was let loose and Saul Farro pulled Balum from the saddle and dumped him to the ground with a thump. With one of his massive hands he reached down and took Balum by the underarm and dragged him several yards off and dropped him.

'Go ahead. Do your business.'

'Untie my feet,' croaked Balum.

A boot struck him in the ribs and rolled him.

'Shut your goddamn mouth. Open it again and the next kick is aimed at your face.'

Balum did as he was told and when he had pulled his trousers back on, difficult as it was with his hands and feet tied together, Saul dragged him back to where the men had built a campfire and threw him to the ground. He landed on his hip, which should have caused his gun to dig into his body, but the Dragoon was gone. He checked with his hands but the holster was empty.

He lay in silence. His head still rang due to the crack

he had received from the crown moulding. It felt swollen and a slight whine hummed away in his ears. In time he slept. When he woke, the sun had nearly broken the edge of the earth and he lay shivering uncontrollably and covered in dew. Its rays gradually extended out over the plains and where they first shone in the grass several yards from him he rolled until he lay in its warmth and rubbed his hands over his body until the shaking had ceased.

Daylight revealed his captors. Aston, Nelson, and Farro. Also Douglass Crenshaw in his fine clothing, fat and pampered as though he were holding court. Shane Carly sat up from his blankets with his face red and his breathing ragged though it was only morning and he had done no physical labor.

Who he did not expect to see was Sara. But there she was, tending to the pot over the fire. Not one look did she cast his way.

They took their breakfast and offered him nothing. Saul was instructed to check the ropes. He did so, adding a kick to Balum's back for good measure. When their food was eaten and the coffee drunk, they threw him again over the roan and bound his hands to his feet. The riders departed out from the dimple of land where they had camped the night and rode north through oceans of swaying grass and stands of oak and pine and cottonwoods thrust upward like islands in that mighty expanse.

All that day they rode under a windless sky. Clouds passed overhead, but none drifted to block the sun burning large and heavy above them. The rustle of leather and hoofbeats sounded loudly in the otherwise silent arena. They met no one coming or going from any place whatsoever, as if the world had emptied itself of human life.

By the edge of a narrow stream they stopped to water the horses. Balum turned his head and looked past the roan's shoulder to where the men knelt with their canteens outstretched. Nelson lifted his dripping from the water and as he drank, his eyes saw Balum watching him. He stood, took another swallow, and approached the roan.

'How's it feel, eh Balum? Chest sore yet? Head hurt?'

Balum's eyes turned to the ground. His ribs were pushed flat against the saddle and his back hurt from the unnatural curve his body held, tied over the saddle as it was.

Nelson reached him and gripped a wad of Balum's hair in his hand and jerked back, cranking Balum's neck backward and lifting his face up. With his free hand he formed a fist and drove it into Balum's face. Blood burst under the crunch of knuckles. It ran from Balum's nose over his lips and dribbled down his chin. When Nelson let his head fall back so his chin rested against the horse's flank, the blood pooled backwards up Balum's nose, causing him to snort and cough and gasp for breath.

'He better not still be bleeding when we get to my place,' whined Shane Carly. 'I don't want blood everywhere.'

'Cut it out, Frederick,' barked Aston from the riverbank.

'I'm just having some fun.'

'Have your fun later. You smash his face in and no one will recognize him. What'll be the point of that?'

The party remounted and crossed the stream. Northward they rode. Only one thing lay ahead of them and that was Cheyenne. Balum's chest rubbed painfully against the saddle. He wondered to himself what plan they had for him. It was not to kill him, that was certain. At least not immediately. His mind ran over the possibilities but came up with nothing.

In the evening they ran through the same motions as before. Balum was thrown to the ground, his bindings secured, and left to shiver in the cold of the coming evening. The rest built a fire and ate. They slept under blankets, and as their snores rose above the sounds of crickets, Balum calculated how many he might kill with his hands before the rest woke and shot him. After several minutes of such thought he admitted to himself that, tied and bound as he was, it was only a fantasy, and he closed his eyes and slept while his stomach grumbled in hunger.

The ground they covered the following day was ground Balum knew well. He had ridden the same plains and ascended the same mesas several times over from Denver to Cheyenne. The CW ranch lay not far off.

They drew close enough to Cheyenne to become wary of other travelers. Saul rode ahead to scout, and more than once he rode back with warnings of riders in the distance. They would stop in the shade of trees and wait until the path was clear. Once, when no cover was to be found, they gagged Balum's mouth and threw him into a shallow cut in the earth and threw debris over him. When the danger had passed they hauled him back out and over the saddle and rode on as before.

An afternoon of hard riding took them within a few miles of Cheyenne. They reined in the horses and dismounted. Talk started up amongst them immediately.

'*This* is where you live?' Sara's voice did not hide her disgust.

'You'll like it,' said Shane Carly. 'It stays cool inside.'

'How long do we have to stay here?' said Sara.

'Not any longer than we need to,' was Aston's reply.

When Balum was jerked off the saddle he stood unbalanced and looked at where they had arrived. The horses stood in a patch of trees that had grown up alongside a hill cut sharply away by the forces of nature. A crooked door hung on a makeshift frame in the flat drop-off of the slope. Trash lay scattered about the entranceway. Broken shards of glass bottles, bean cans strewn about the mud and half rusted out. Saul and Aston each took an arm and hauled Balum inside. The rest followed.

The smell of dust and stale earth greeted them. Balum landed with a thump against the dirt wall cut deep into the hillside. The darkness was lessened by an oil lamp Shane Carly was quick to light. It revealed only two rooms; the main room which held a table, a few chairs and a straw mattress, and a small adjoining room where a type of stove had been fashioned up and a hole dug up through the hilltop to release cooking smoke.

'Make yourselves at home, boys,' said Shane Carly. 'And you as well, ma'am,' he added to Sara with a ridiculous smile.

The girl looked around, appalled at her surroundings.

'Let me offer you all some whiskey,' said Shane. 'This is the best stuff in all of Colorado and the Wyoming Territory.'

Aston and Crenshaw refused, knowing full well the quality of the poison swill Shane Carly sold under the name of whiskey. Saul and Nelson happily accepted two mugs. The first greedy sips were immediately replaced by expressions of disgust.

'What is this shit?' yelled Nelson.

'That's good corn whiskey right there,' said Shane.

'Tastes like you've let dog piss ferment.'

'Aw, come on. It's not that bad.'

'You don't need to be drinking it anyway,' said Aston. 'There's work to do.'

'How far away is the ranch?' said Nelson.

'A few miles.'

'Good. I don't feel like riding much more. So what's the plan? Get them in the morning?'

'No. The train doesn't come in until the day after tomorrow. We'll wait until tomorrow night. The less time they're missing, the better for us.'

'What are we supposed to do until then?' asked Sara.

'Whatever you want. Just stay here and out of sight.'

Balum listened, slouched on the floor against the wall.

'We gonna tell this bum what he's in for?' asked

Nelson.

They all turned to where Balum lay tied up. Crenshaw snorted.

'He might as well know now,' said Aston, looking at Balum. 'You're going to do us a great service, Balum. Consider it repayment for putting my brother through such tribulations.'

Balum's eyes cut over to Nelson. Charles had been right. So had Daniel and Chester. He thought of Caesar Costas from the cantina and waited for the rest to come. His fears did not go unvindicated.

'All of Denver has serious doubts about you now, Balum. Any more problems you give 'em and they'll be ready to hang you. They just need a little push. Well, we're gonna give you that push.'

'What the hell are you talking about?' said Balum.

'Balum the great train robber. That's what I'm talking about. The cattle payload comes in once a month from Kansas City. We've gone after it twice but luck hasn't been on our side. Once the wrong train, once the wrong date. But now we know. The day after tomorrow, on the ten sixty-five, over sixty thousand dollars will be riding in a strong box located in the car behind the steam engine. Enough to buy thousands of head of fat cattle. But that money has a better destination.'

'Damn right it does,' Frederick Nelson slammed his glass down.

'What have I got to do with this?' said Balum.

'Why, you're robbing that train right along with us,

149

Balum. You're going to be known from here to Texas as the man who robbed the ten sixty-five.'

'You're out of your mind. Sounds like you're drunk off that dog piss whiskey.' Balum pulled his feet up and straightened his back against the dirt wall. 'Why would I do that? If it's between helping you or getting shot, I'd rather be shot. I'm no thief.'

'We figured as much. That's why we're not threatening to shoot you.'

Balum looked at his captors in the heavy air weighed down with dust and lit weakly by the oil lamp. Saul and Frederick grinned with their whiskey mugs in hand.

'We'll shoot your friends, Balum,' said Aston. 'Just think of that poor boy's new bride, and how sad and lonely she'll be when her new husband is found with his head cut off in a manure pile. And that Mexican woman's bawling when she discovers her man has met the same fate.'

Balum said nothing. He thought of Charles and Will and what a fool he had been to bring the Sandersons to the wedding.

'We'll bring them back here tomorrow night. We'll have them tied up just as pretty as you are now, and the day following we'll ride out each one of us, Sara here to mind your friends, and we'll take all sixty thousand dollars off that train. And you'll be the face they see. You can say no, Balum. Just remember. If you do, it won't only be your neck on the line.'

# 18

They rode out the following afternoon, four men armed like cavalry and bent on a hellish mission. Sara stood in the doorway and watched them leave, then walked about aimlessly in the yard by the horses after they'd left.

Shane Carly sat at the table sipping his own putrid whiskey and watching her through the doorway. He had filled a bowl with shards of beef jerky and he munched on pieces of the dried beef while his small eyes squinted into the sunlight after her. When the whiskey was finished he stood with the bowl of jerked meat and paced over the dirt floor of the cramped and musty room, peering out the doorway at each pass.

'I think she likes me,' he said after a while.

'Sara?' Balum was incredulous.

'Good looking women are attracted to good looking men.'

'You're a fool.'

Shane turned and looked at Balum. His mouth worked over the jerky. A piece fell from his hand and landed in the dirt but he made no move to retrieve it.

'Do you know what you're doing tangled up with these

151

guys?' said Balum. 'They're using you. When they're through they'll kill you. Or they'll figure something worse for you.'

'They like me,' argued Shane. 'And I like them. They're tough. They're winners. And I'm a winner. That's all there is in life; winners and losers. And look at yourself, tied up there on the floor. You think I'd team up with you? Ha.'

He turned away from the fallen piece of beef and stood in the doorway longing for the woman outside. Sporadically he would swing his head back around to check on Balum, then drift back into ignorant fantasies of how he might win over Sara's love. When his little mind had landed on a path forward he left the doorway and approached her where she stood in the shade by the horses.

Balum sat alone on the dirt floor and waited for Shane's figure to disappear. He leaned forward and began to work at the ropes wound about his ankles. His fingers dug into them. He pulled and pried, but after several minutes it became apparent that the ropes were tied so tight they would need to be cut off. He let himself fall back to the wall and stared at his boots. Suddenly his hands moved to his breast pocket. He patted it and felt for the envelope underneath.

It was still there, waiting.

Sunlight came through the open doorway. Shane's high-pitched voice drifted far away outside. Balum drew the envelope from his pocket and looked at the writing. His breath came heavy. One more look outside. Emptiness. He slipped a finger through the flap and ripped it open. The paper inside had been folded once in half. He opened it and read the words in the musty filth of Shane Carly's dugout.

*Dear Balum,*

*My heart jumped when I received your letter. I had not expected it and when it was given to me I realized how deeply I missed your words, your presence. You must have wondered why I did not meet you that night at the station. I would have, gladly, but the letter was not delivered to me until the day after you left it. Natasha is not the most reliable of my girls.*

*I've thought a lot about what you might have said to me there that night, had I met you. I've also spent time thinking of what I might say to you the next time we meet.*

*I love you, Balum. I've loved you since the first day I saw you, sitting ragged and bloody at my barroom table. I know what I've said to you before has been harsh. It's true, I still believe, that you and I are untamed souls. We are wild creatures that live outside the parameters of society. I used this as an excuse to not settle down. I told myself you would hurt me, or worse yet, that I would hurt you. But I realize now those worries are not strong enough to keep me from wanting you.*

*I know what you're searching for, Balum. You've made it clear, through your own way. I want what I believe you want. I want us to be together.*

*I hope this letter finds you soon. I have no doubt you will be present at Will's wedding. I will be there too. My Uncle Roger will be with me, I'll be happy for you to meet him. Until then I'll think of you and wish you well.*

*Love,*
*Angelique*

Balum took a sharp breath. He folded the letter quickly and shoved it back into his breast pocket. Pressure welled inside his skull. He'd been such a fool. He knew all along who it was he dreamed would share that ranch house with in his imagination. Who would be the mother of the children running in the yard. His own fears had kept him from that. Fears of rejection. Of the inability to provide what she might need.

He bent forward again and struggled at the ropes binding his ankles together. Nothing moved. His thoughts turned to Charles and Will. They were no tinhorns. They'd seen their share of gunbattles. And it wasn't just them. That bunkhouse they'd built could house two dozen men, and Balum knew they were filling it with tough, reliable hombres. Still, he worried. Bound as he was and unable to move, those worries grew at him. His mind worked frantically. Shane was still outside. He needed to find something to cut the ropes.

He rolled to his hands and knees and began to worm his way over the dirt to the kitchen. Cockroaches crawled over the floor in front of him. He rose to his knees and looked about for a knife. Footsteps hit the dirt behind him and Shane Carly let out a yelp.

'Hey! Get back here.'

The pudgy man grabbed Balum awkwardly by the arm and Balum pushed from his feet and rammed his skull into Shane Carly's face. The man fell in a soft pile of flesh and Balum turned back to the kitchen. Alongside the stove two knives sat, covered in dried grease and food. He took the larger of the two and bent to his ankles.

Shane Carly moaned beside him. If he rose, Balum decided, he'd plunge the knife into the man's soft neck. The determination found no waiver to it, but the sound of a hammer cocking back was the unseen force that finally stopped Balum's feverish hacking at the ropes.

Sara stood in the dim light of the adjoining room with her eyes looking down the barrel of a Colt model 1860 revolver.

'You'd shoot me?' he asked her.

'I'll start with a bullet in the leg. We still need you for the train. But yes, I'd shoot you. Don't doubt it.'

'So it was all for the money? That's it?'

'Ten thousand is no small sum. They say a fool and his money are soon separated. I spotted you for a fool the moment I saw you. I'll admit,' she let her eyes roam down his body, 'I had a good time doing it. I think you did as well. Now put that knife down and get back into this room. Shane, get up.'

Balum inched his way back over the dirt to his space against the wall. Shane was slow to pick himself off the ground.

'Check his ropes again,' said Sara. 'I don't know why those idiots didn't tie his hands behind his back.'

'They couldn't have tied him over the horse that way.'

'Shut up, Shane. Just check the ropes.'

When Shane had finished his inspection of Balum's feet and ankles he sat at the table across from Sara. Balum sat against the sod wall in the darkening stink of the room. A mouse appeared out of the kitchen. It watched Balum, looked at the two at the table, and summoned the courage to enter. It finally did, running past his feet and snatching up the piece of jerked meat still lying on the dirt floor.

Shadows stretched out away from the setting sun. Shane piped up at times. He bragged about his whiskey. His company was requested everywhere he went, he insisted. Responses from Sara were sparse.

The riders returned before nightfall. Sara jumped from the table and stood in the doorway watching the men dismount under the trees. Shane rose and looked over her shoulder from behind.

'Where are they?' she said as the four approached the dugout.

They filed in, faces tight and shoulders hunched.

'Uncle Frederick?' she asked, turning to Nelson.

'Let your father explain it. It was his harebrained idea.'

'Father?'

Aston took his hat off and threw it on the table. 'Give me some of that goddamn piss-whiskey,' he barked.

'What happened?' Sara demanded to anyone who would answer.

'It's a fortress,' said Saul. 'That's what happened. There's over a dozen cowhands riding all around the place, half of them Mexican, each one loaded down with weaponry like they were going off to war. One of those Mexes had a set of bandoliers strapped across his damn chest. Ain't no four men gonna drag anyone out of there.'

'What will you do now?' she asked.

'I'm thinking on it,' said Aston between gulps of whiskey.

'Thinking on it? It looks like you're trying to get drunk to me.'

'Leave me be.'

'Let's just shoot him,' said Crenshaw. 'It would have been hard enough to get him to cooperate with the robbery even if we had been able to hold his friends as hostages.'

'Then who will they pin the robbery on?' said Nelson.

Crenshaw shrugged. His lawyer brain was through lawyering.

'I got an idea,' said Saul. 'Those two friends he's always hanging around with in Denver. One's an old man, the other doesn't even carry a gun. It'll be easy.'

'The train comes in tomorrow,' said Nelson. 'No way we can get to Denver and back before then.'

'Shoot him,' Crenshaw suggested for the second time.

Shane Carly's head turned to each man as they spoke, this way and that. He poured more whiskey into Aston's glass and held the bottle out for anyone else who would dare accept it. Gradually, he found takers, and all but Sara stood or sat at the table with rancid whiskey coating their tongues.

'There's a better idea.'

Each man turned his head to Sara.

'There's a woman,' she said. 'I know the way a man looks at a woman, and I saw the way he looked at her.'

'Who?' said Aston.

'She was at the wedding. Dark hair, mid thirties, attractive. Beautiful, really.'

'Yes, but *who*?'

'I don't know who she is, but she's out there.'

Frederick Nelson slammed his whiskey glass over the table and stood up. He picked his hat up and pulled it over his dome. 'If you know what she looks like, I know where to find her.'

'Tell us what you know, Frederick,' said Aston.

'When Balum took me in, we didn't go directly to Denver. We made a detour here to Cheyenne. He had somebody he wanted to meet. Stayed out all night at the train station waiting, but that person never showed. What do you think he did then? He rode up to a whore house and peeked in the door. Whatever he saw he didn't like. The whore was probably with some fella. But that's who it is. I'd lay my money on it.'

'You're telling us he's in love with a whore?' Crenshaw said in disbelief. 'One he'd rob a train for?'

'I saw it,' Aston cut in. 'I saw that same woman at the wedding. You're right, Sara. He didn't take his eyes off her from the moment it started. Frederick, can you find that whore house?'

'I'll find it.'

Aston pushed the whiskey away. 'Saddle up boys. We're riding.'

# 19

They returned two hours later in whoops and hollers, as though the bit of whiskey they had drunk had delayed its effects and descended upon them in that instant more powerful and intoxicating than anticipated. Boots stomped over the grassless yard before the dugout. Shane Carly swung the door wide and ran outside, taking the oil lamp with him and leaving Balum and Sara in the pitch black.

Angelique was the first to enter. Her dress immaculate. Hair dark and shining. Rope wound about her arms, restricting them against her ribs.

Frederick Nelson pushed her forward through the doorway and into the filth of Shane Carly's home. Her face turned in the dark, searching to make sense of her kidnapper's ambitions. It took a moment for her eyes to adjust to the gloomy interior. Balum could see her features. She was scared, there was no mistaking it, yet she was composed, sure of herself as always.

'Go ahead,' grunted Nelson. 'Have a seat over there by your sweetheart.'

Her eyes found him. Eyes frightened and silent. She walked to the wall and turned and sat with her back to it,

Balum beside her. The two looked at each other in the darkness, their eyes connecting through the haze of dirty air, and Balum knew there was no rancor in her heart. Guilt rose up within him. He wished to speak his mind to her but he knew not what to say, nor was the moment given to him.

'Why don't we take her to the trees outside and have some fun?' said Saul. 'She won't mind. She's nothing but a whore anyway.'

'You hear that, Balum?' said Nelson. 'Saul wants to have a little fun. I bet Shane does too. And Crenshaw. Hell, we could hump her till sunup. I expect you wouldn't like that much.'

Balum kept his lips together.

'That's what I thought. So I'll tell you what. Tonight she can sit right there next to you. But hear me clear. You don't help us on that train tomorrow and that whore of yours won't be able to walk, come tomorrow evening.'

Shane Carly had entered with the oil lamp.

'Time to get some shuteye, boys,' said Aston. 'We'll be leaving at sunup tomorrow. Spread your blankets and take a shot of whiskey if it'll help you sleep.'

'I'd rather sleep outside,' said Sara.

'Suit yourself,' said Aston. 'But you're taking first watch over these two. Shane'll take second. Hear that, Shane?'

'I hear it.'

'They're tied good enough. Let 'em sleep. But they start moving around too much, or they stand up, club 'em down. I'd rather not have you shoot them. We didn't got to all this work for nothing. Now turn out that light.'

They had taken their bedrolls from the horses and unfurled them over the dirt floor. Shane extinguished the flame and darkness swept over the room, gradually eased by the shimmer of stars through the one small window. Balum and Angelique shimmied down the wall until they were off it, their bodies flat over the floor. They lied close together, facing each other with the warmth of their breath mixing. Snores rippled out around them.

'What's happening, Balum?' Angelique's voice reached him so quietly it was barely a whisper.

'They want me to rob the train with them tomorrow.'

'Why?'

'So they can pin it on me. Nelson's trial was a circus. They found him innocent. Half of Denver already thinks I should hang from the stories they told about me. If people think I robbed the train, these boys won't have a thing to worry about.'

'So that's why they brought me here. To make you do it.'

They were quiet for a moment. Two invisible faces in the dark. Angelique leaned closer to him, her lips nearly brushing his cheek.

'It won't do any good, Balum. They'll kill you afterwards.'

'They'll kill me if I don't. That's certain,' he whispered, scarcely audible. He ached to reach a hand out to her, to touch her, wrap her close against him. 'I'm sorry,' he said finally.

'It's not your fault.'

'I'm sorry for everything else. I was angry with you. I didn't read your letter until just today. I got mixed up with that girl Sara and turned a deaf ear to my friends' warnings. I love you Angelique. Always have.'

She leaned forward until her nose grazed his own. Her hands, bound by rope, reached out and found Balum's and she held his fingers in hers. 'I knew I wanted you ever since I first saw you sitting in my barroom looking like you'd been dragged through hell. I just tried not to admit it.'

'I'm going to make sure every one of them winds up dead or in jail. I just don't know how.'

'You'll have to think of something quickly, Balum. Robbing the train with them will buy you time, but not much. After that they'll kill us both.'

Outside the wind had picked up. An owl called out somewhere far away.

'I know it,' he mouthed the words. 'I know it.'

# 20

Six men they were, horses galloping under them with necks stretched out to the rising sun. From afar there was no sound to them, only specks on the plains, dust hanging in the air where they passed. For the riders clustered tight, their ears were filled with the clink of metal on harnesses, the stomping of hooves over a trembling earth. They rode as though cornets played above them, drowning out the silence of the flat empty land before them.

Their path cut well south of Cheyenne. No one saw the dust rise. No one heard the horses' hooves nor the squeak of leather against leather. No cornets trumpeted their movements.

Balum's body held stiff in the saddle atop the roan. At every mile he searched for the chance of escape. The men riding with him allowed him no opportunity. They rode on all sides of him, their eyes watchful. He thought of Angelique left alone and tied in the dugout with Sara standing guard over her. He imagined her death, and his, their graves or lack thereof, and battled these thoughts from his mind.

Having passed Cheyenne they curved to the northeast

along hardpack of little resource to the withered grasses that grew thin and weak, gasping up toward the sky. The soil turned from loam to sand to clay. Plant life grew only in patches. Mesas rose in tight mounds above them, towering a hundred feet into the air or more. The hooves churned up dust which billowed around them and the riders pulled bandanas of varying colors over their mouths and noses and squinted their eyes as they trotted toward the glistening rail tracks ahead.

No one spoke through that long ride. Sweat stained their clothing as the sun heated the humid air. It trickled from their brows and into the bandanas, cutting minuscule rivers through their dust-caked faces. Revolver handles protruded form holsters. Colts and Remingtons and Manhattan Navys. Cords of rope hung looped from saddle pommels. Rope destined to pull the strongbox from the traincar should the need arise.

After three hours of hard riding, the horses were worked into a lather and the men wet with sweat and covered in dust and grime. They followed the rails east until they saw the hot iron tracks curve sharply to the south over their massive wooden ties. On careful steps they crossed the rails and rode to the shadowed floor at the foot of a towering mesa and pulled their horses to a stop. Sand cherry and sagebrush grew in ragged clumps. Among the thirsty shrubs the riders dismounted and drank long and greedily at their canteens. They offered Balum nothing.

'What's the matter, Balum?' taunted Nelson. 'Thirsty?'

Shane Carly laughed along at the bigman's joke.

'Listen up boys,' said Aston. 'When she comes around that bend she's gonna have to slow down. That'll be our chance. But no foolishness; she'll still be coming in hot. Once we board, you keep those bandanas snug over your faces. I don't care how hot your damn breath is underneath. Frederick, you and me will head straight for the engine. We'll stop the train, and if that lockbox doesn't open easy we'll pull the goddamn thing off with rope. Shane, that means you need to have those horses rounded up and alongside the train. I want that rope handy. Got that?'

'Sure,' he said, his face sweating and his eyes showing their whites.

'Saul, Douglas, you two make sure no passengers get any wild ideas. Keep your guns on them. Take their wallets and purses and if you see any watches or jewelry you might as well grab that up as well. Use that burlap sack we brought. And you damn well better keep an eye on Balum. Keep your gun on him as much as anyone else. Which reminds me,' Aston reached into the saddlebag on his horse's flank and brandished Balum's Dragoon. 'I suppose you'll be wanting this back.'

Balum caught it in the air. From the weight he knew immediately the chambers had been emptied.

'It's empty,' he said.

'No shit it's empty,' said Saul.

'It'll stay empty. Once this is all over with you can have your whore back and go buy as many bullets as you please.'

Balum holstered the gun and looked down the tracks.

There would be nothing after this. Not in those men's plan.

The sun drifted in the sky. The edge of the mesa's shadow crept closer to them and they hugged tighter to the rising cliff to keep from the sun's heat. Saul walked about picking up stones and throwing them. Douglas Crenshaw and Shane Carly sweated as though the cool of the shade had no effect on them. A hawk flew overhead, circled, disappeared.

'And one more thing,' said Aston suddenly. 'Don't any of you fools go using each other's names. Got that?'

They mumbled and bobbed their heads.

The sun cut over the peak of the mesa and burned away the shadow with it. They stood in the sun with their eyes squinting under their hat brims and waited.

The smudge of thick steam rising like a tendril up to the sky was what they saw before they heard any sound, any grinding of wheels, the pump of the engine. It came rocketing out of the southeast, gleaming in the sunlight, red and black and thunderous.

'Wait till she's just past us!' shouted Aston.

It slowed and took the bend, turning to show each railcar linked one after another. When the engine had reached the straightaway toward Cheyenne Aston glanced back and motioned with his hand and they took off all six of them once more, charging like cavalry into war. The last of the cars with the caboose attached at the end slipped round the bend and the horses turned in line with the squealing cars, their feet matching the velocity of the train. Dust rose in a haze about them. Aston and Nelson shouted commands which were swept away before they could be heard. Nelson was the first to board the train. He grabbed the metal railing of the caboose end and flipped a leg over the saddle, then jumped from the stirrup and landed on his knees on the platform.

Aston rode alongside Balum. He pulled his gun and leveled it across his saddle and shouted words which Balum couldn't hear but knew full well their intention. He charged the roan over the extended railroad ties and performed the same movements Nelson had, his mind reeling when his eyes caught the ground flying past beneath. With a hand clutching the railing, Balum leapt from the roan. Nelson grabbed him by the shoulders as he landed and pulled him onto the clear section of platform. Aston followed. Saul charged in behind him, the train beginning to accelerate on the straightaway. He jumped, caught the railing, and landed with his legs crashing into the metal staircase. His horse veered wildly away from the commotion and Shane Carly's figure shrunk as he scrambled in the blowing dust to round up the horses.

Crenshaw came charging behind. His eyes were wild and the bandana had fallen away from his face. The horse beneath him flared its nostrils, sides heaving with the load of the fatman on its back. Crenshaw reached out a hand in an empty gesture.

'Get closer!' shouted Aston from the caboose's stairway. 'Pull your leg over!'

Crenshaw waved his hand pathetically while his horse lagged further behind.

'Goddamnit!' Aston yelled again, but Crenshaw's horse had flagged, and the train drew away.

'He'll catch up to us when we stop,' shouted Nelson above the train whistle. 'Let's go.'

Through the caboose the four men walked. The crew's accommodations were stacked against the car walls. A small table with remains of food sat uncleaned. They crossed the distance outside to the next car, bandanas covering each face save for Balum's. Under each bandana their hands clutched guns, hammers cocked back. The door swung open and they made their way through an aisle packed tight with chests and boxes and supplies packed up from distant places. Frederick Nelson led the way, Balum behind him. Saul and Aston took up the rear.

'Pull your gun out, Balum,' Aston ordered from the back.

Balum did as he was told. His mind scrambled for a solution but nothing came of it.

The next two cars held more of the same. Balum swung his eyes over his surroundings, looking for a weapon of any sort. Something he could use as a club, anything. All about him the supplies sat wrapped in rope or packed tightly away in crates and chests. They crossed to the next car, the next after that. On the following they ripped open the door to a passenger car with two rows of benches all facing them.

Nelson raised his gun barrel at the shocked faces. 'Put your hands up, each one of you. Raise them up high or take a bullet.'

Ladies in long dresses sat closest. Behind them were businessmen in broadcloth suits and a family with three young boys. At the far end sat two buffalo hunters with long beards and hollow eyes and two Sharps Model 1853's laid up against the window.

'You two boys just leave those rifles where they lay,' said Nelson. He turned to Aston behind him. 'Ast... I mean...you. Let's go.'

Aston moved up from behind, and as he came abreast of Balum he addressed the passengers.

'Ladies and gentlemen, this, most clearly, is a robbery. I'll ask you to kindly hand over your valuables to the gentlemen in the rear,' he motioned to Saul, 'including banknotes, purses, watches and jewelry. I'll take this opportunity to ensure you that if you produce a weapon or interfere with our actions in any way, we will shoot you. Do not doubt it.'

He looked around at the eyes peering back at his masked face, then continued.

'And when you've reached Cheyenne and they ask you who robbed the train, you can tell them it was the great train thief Balum!'

At this he swung a hand up to Balum's uncovered face. The passengers gawked and stared. Balum stood motionless, the unloaded Dragoon hanging from his hand. Aston pushed him forward to the next car and repeated the same message to the collection of frightened passengers huddled together. Nelson went on ahead to the engine, and when Saul came through the door Aston departed to the front.

Balum watched as Saul made the rounds collecting valuables. He stood over a thin man with a crooked lip that quivered when Saul held out the burlap sack for his wallet. The thin man carried no gun. He drew his wallet from his breast pocket and dropped it gingerly into the sack, then placed his hand back at his side and shied away from the bandit as if he feared being struck.

In the engine room Nelson laid the barrel of his revolver alongside the conductor's head and let him know in clear terms what his fate should be if the train did not stop immediately. The conductor threw the break. A grinding sound shrieked from the rails and the train shuddered to a stop. Within seconds Douglas Crenshaw's sweating mass of fat boarded the train and waddled into the passenger car where Balum and Saul stood.

'Help me fill this sack,' barked Saul.

Crenshaw drew his gun and wiggled it at the paralyzed passengers. His other hand he held extended to receive gifts like a deacon circulating an offering bowl. When the riders had been fleeced of their valuables, Saul and Crenshaw urged Balum forward through the door and out onto the metal deck platforms. They crossed the space in the open air and threw wide the door on the end of the next car.

Saul entered first. Not but one foot had crossed into the car when a bullet smashed into the wood a few inches to the left of his head. Saul's gun was already out. The passenger who had fired the shot held his smoking revolver before him, his face a contortion of frightened horror which was soon erased by a lead projectile that blew through his forehead and sprayed the contents within that cranium over the seatbacks and passengers throughout the traincar.

Saul swung his gun over the rest.

'Anyone else feel like shooting?' he shouted. 'The next idiot who tries that will get his head blown off just the same. I'll do it, or maybe Balum will do it.'

The door on the far end of the car swung open and Aston leaned through.

'What happened?' he bellowed, but the destruction was clear to see. Blood and bits of brain and skull streaked the walls and windows and had speckled the faces and clothing of the men and women seated about.

'You,' Aston pointed at Saul. 'We can't get the strongbox open. Get some rope from outside and we'll pull it out. Take Balum with you. And you,' he looked at Crenshaw. 'Get the rest of the valuables until the train starts moving again.'

Outside, Shane Carly had rounded up the horses. He sat with them, his small eyes squinting in the sunlight and his mouth open and quivering slightly.

When Saul reached the horses he mounted his own and lifted a coil of rope from the pommel of another. Balum put a foot in the stirrup and swung up on top of the roan. Shane Carly glanced at him but said nothing. Saul had already begun to ride forward to the car holding the strongbox.

'It's on the other side,' shouted Aston with his head stuck out the traincar window. 'Ride around.'

In the growing confusion of the separation, Balum saw his chance. He reached for the remaining coil of rope and laid it across his lap. Shane Carly sat stupidly next to him.

'Stay here,' Balum ordered.

Shane should have refused. He should have drawn a gun on Balum, shouted out for help, anything. But Shane Carly was a fool. Used to taking orders from the strongmen he aspired to be one day, he took the order silently from Balum; a man who in his subconscious he knew to be the most strong-willed of them all.

Saul had already circled around the front of the steam engine and crossed the tracks to the other side. Balum followed. He crossed over the railroad ties and on the other side he paused at the steam engine window. The conductor stood watching, his hands hanging helpless at his sides.

'Start this train moving again,' said Balum.

'That big feller said I ain't to do that till ya'll have up and left.'

'I'm telling you now. Lock the engine door and get this thing moving.'

The conductor disappeared into the engine room. Balum led the roan out from the tracks and down to the second car where Saul had thrown one end of the rope through a window. Inside, Nelson and Aston were busy tying it about the strongbox.

A lethargic chug bellowed from the engine chimney

and the crankshafts jerked the driving wheels into motion.

'The train's moving!' Saul yelled out the obvious.

'Let her move,' Aston piped back. 'Take out the slack in that rope and start pulling.'

Saul backed his horse up and the rope snapped taut.

'Pull it, Goddamn you!' Aston yelled from the traincar window.

Saul pulled, and as he did so the train picked up speed, the cylinders and pistons grinding louder and steam huffing from the boiler and shooting out from fissures in the water tanks.

Balum grabbed one end of the rope over his pommel and tied a loose overhand knot through which he rethreaded the tail end. He tightened it, passed through the slack, and tied on a stopper knot. With the lasso tied, he gripped the loop in his right hand and turned the roan.

The strongbox had shimmied up the wall to the window and Saul's horse began to lose ground as the tension on the rope increased. Balum edged the roan up to Saul's rear. The man's attention was focused only on the rope and the shouting coming from inside the traincar. The strongbox strained against the window frame, buckling the wooden bracings. Aston and Nelson had begun to kick and pound at the frame, weakening it for the box to break through.

Balum whipped the lasso overhead. Many a month he had labored as a cowhand. He had thrown rope over countless cattle. Rope during branding, rope thrown over calves stuck in mud wallows. He let it fly from his hand and the rope looped over Saul's torso. Balum pulled it tight with a jerk. The motion snapped the slack from the noose and winched the man's arms against his ribs and he turned with his eyes wild and surprised. The horse underneath skipped forward under the pull of the rope still attached to the strongbox in the train.

Balum tugged in the opposite direction, toward the caboose end, and Saul's own rope pulling at the strongbox sprang loose from the saddle horn. The strongbox crashed back down to the floor of the car and the rope attached to it skipped freely over the railroad ties as the train chugged down the tracks.

Nelson, Aston and Crenshaw ran for the exits as the train gathered speed. They spilled out into the dust where Shane Carly sat in complete ignorance of what had happened on the opposite side of the train.

Saul bent his forearm for the gun in his holster but his arms were smashed tight against his ribs. Balum had reached the caboose. He trotted the roan alongside of it and threw the rope over the iron railing, caught the loose end, and tied a double knot linking the rope fast to the train.

The engine spit steam from its chimney far ahead. The caboose had caught up with Saul and as it slid past, the two sides of the tracks came into view of each other again. On the opposite side, Aston, Nelson and Crenshaw ran on foot to their horses.

Saul kicked his horse with his heels. His eyes stared at the lasso noose connecting his body with the end of the train as though it were some unreckonable power to which he had been subjected. Balum rode with him, and the two horses broke into a run as the train puffed and wheezed and cranked its wheels along the rail irons. Behind them the rest of the party had regained their mounts and took off after the train.

The horses were put to a canter, and as the crankshafts found their motion and the train barreled forward, Saul beat his heels into the horse's flanks until he was galloping at top speed, the slack in the rope slowly tightening out. He shouted something at Balum that was lost in the noise of the train, and as the slack disappeared from the rope he kicked furiously at his flagging horse until the beast could maintain its speed no longer, and suddenly, like a fish being plucked from water, Saul Farro was lifted out of the saddle. There was a moment where he coasted through the air, then hit the ground in a smack. A plume of dust exploded and a heavy cloud was kicked up into the air by Saul's massive body being drug through the hardpack clay behind the train. His screams were lost to the roar of the train. The friction of the ground beneath him tore quickly through his jeans, his jacket. Pieces of clothing were ripped and strewn behind him, leaving his skin to scrape along the jagged ground below, bouncing over the protruding iron rails and drug over railroad ties and stone. The skin peeled away from his body, blood and muscle and bone to follow. Along the railroad ties for half a mile, Saul Farro's body was wiped like a soiled rag, leaving nothing but a dark red streak staining a line of gore behind the receding traincars.

When his body had been thoroughly obliterated there was nothing left but the rope skipping whimsically behind the caboose and the long whistle of steam piping through the engine chimney.

# 21

Balum bent low over the roan's neck. His pursuers lagged at a distance of no more than a hundred yards. Gunshots rang out behind him. Balls of lead whistled through the air and into nowhere.

Douglas Crenshaw was the first to give up. He was no horseman, and the steed he rode, though determined, was not built to carry such a load on its back in an all-out charge. Shane Carly was next. His panting had become as ragged as his horse's, and he veered off away from the building cloud of dust and sat staring ahead with his mouth hanging open and his beady eyes squinting into the sun.

Frederick Nelson and Aston Sanderson rode side by side, horse legs drumming the earth underneath. They rode solid horses, but both men were by nature large and heavy. Too much time had passed since they had been given cause to expel such effort. They fired more shots at Balum's shrinking figure and slowed to a canter. Nelson swung his head around and shouted at the two laggards behind him with an accompanying wave of his revolver. They could not catch him, but neither would he escape their sight. If he did it was no matter; they all knew where he was headed.

Balum's roan knew when it was time to run. It had carried the same man on its back nearly all its life and could feel the urgency in the way Balum leaned forward, the clamp of his legs along its ribs. Its hooves clawed forward in massive strides, forelegs pounding the earth and the thighs and rump launching it forward anew. They rode out of the harsh clay sand and into the darker ground where grass sprouted and grew and waved in sheets before them.

He looked behind him several times to gauge the distance between himself and his pursuers. The line he took toward Shane Carly's pitiful dugout was more direct than the route they had ridden that same morning. His mind scrambled for a plan. Sara would be waiting, her gun as well. He had no doubt she would use it. Nothing came to him. He was a man who needed time to wrestle a problem down, time to ponder it with a wad of tobacco in his cheek in the shade of a tree. Time he did not have.

Nearing the hill that encased Shane Carly's hovel he looked back again. A mile, no more, separated him from the men. A few minute's time was what he had to retrieve Angelique without one or both of them being shot. It occurred to him to swing wide of the dugout, climb the hill and descend on foot to the doorway, but it was too much. They would reach him by then.

As the roan charged forward he realized blankly that he had no plan at all. His mind reeled. Riding head-on

179

would bring Sara out. On a gut feeling he cut south and rode hard to the base of the hillside. When he reached it he swung north again and rode along the edge of the hill at a trot. He could see the trash strewn about the doorway in the distance. The two remaining horses stood in the shade of the trees.

No sign of movement. Fifty yards from the doorway he prodded the roan to a gallop.

The pounding of hooves brought Sara to the doorway. She stepped outside and turned toward the sound of the rider. It took a moment for her mind to register what was happening. A moment too long. When she made the connection that it was Balum charging down upon her she raised the gun in her hand, but he was already there. He drove the horse's shoulder into her, sending her sprawling. Without waiting for the horse to come to a stop he jumped off and tumbled head over heels in the dirt. Sara's gun had gone flying and when he regained his feet he ran for it. Sara had risen. The gun lay closer to her and she reached it first. She bent for it, came up with it and pulled the hammer back but Balum was there. He ripped it from her hands and let the hammer down, then shoved it into his waistband and pushed Sara through the dugout doorway.

Angelique's hands were tied but her feet were not. Unattended, she had already run to the kitchen and found the knife. Balum threw Sara aside and took the knife from Angelique's hands. He sawed the rusted blade furiously against the ropes, but they only frayed and caught in the teeth.

In his mind Balum imagined the thunder of horses closing the distance.

'Get to the horse,' he said, and threw the knife aside.

She ran with her hands still tied in front of her and asked no questions. Balum stepped toward Sara and the girl backed to the corner.

'What do you think you're doing with me?' she hissed.

'You're coming with.'

'Like hell I am.'

He wasted no movement. She swung at him. Her fist struck him in the face but he was against her already. He threw her to a shoulder and carried her outside, then threw her body over his saddle. He climbed on after her, and shoved her forward, then threw her across his lap without any mind paid to her flailing legs and arms.

'Where to?' said Angelique from the saddle.

'The CW.'

She left without a backward look. Balum nudged the roan up to Sara's paint horse and took it up by the reins, then reconsidered. He drew Sara's revolver from his waistband and fired it into the air and struck the horse on its flank. It bolted in the direction it faced; southward and away from where Angelique was already galloping.

Balum followed in her wake.

Sara fought where she lay, but with his free hand Balum pushed her head down along the roan's shoulder and leaned forward, pinning her body against its neck, the saddle horn digging into her ribs. She continued to kick and squirm, which Balum ended by smacking her upturned rump with his open hand. She yelped at the sting of it, but ceased her fighting.

The roan had enjoyed no more than a couple minute's rest at the dugout. The added weight of the girl over its back slowed its steps. Its head lolled and its ribs heaved in search of breath. Balum slowed it to a walk. He hoped Sara's horse would confuse the riders, even if only for a short advantage, though the hope he held was small.

They gained on him, slowly. It was not only their dust he saw. At a half mile out he could see each individual rider. The CW ranch remained a few miles to the north. He continued to walk the roan, giving it all the time he could to gather its breath again. The time would come to sprint. He could always dump Sara from the saddle, though it was a last resort. With her across his lap they would hold their fire.

Beyond that, he needed her for something else. In exactly what capacity, he did not yet know, but she was the link to the men behind him, and though they rode in pursuit they had yet to realize who was the predator and who was the prey. For Balum had reached the end of patience. The end of the law, the courts, the end of reason. He had on his mind two things only: to ensure Angelique's safety, and the bloody lust of revenge.

A shallow ravine opened up and he took it. Behind him the riders had reached the dugout and turned after him. The riderless horse had not fooled them.

The roan scrambled along the moist floor of the ravine and when a cut appeared through the rolling hillside to his left he took it, picking the horse up to a trot again. He rode in clear view of them. They turned one by one into the ravine after him, their horses' hooves trampling through the tracks of the roan.

At the high point of the hill Balum turned and drew Sara's gun from his waistband. He leveled it down at the riders and let off a shot, then another. The distance was too great for accuracy, and the change in elevation complicated the shot. The riders scrambled chaotically, unprepared for gunfire. Balum wasted no more time. He shoved the gun into his belt and let the roan stretch its legs. The ground opened up in a flat plain before him. The house and corrals of the CW ranch sat like small dark smudges on the horizon. The roan ran as though it knew the odds were against it. Its neck stretched forward and it ran in a solid gait, the strides even and firm on the ground.

The details of the CW ranch came into focus. Angelique had already arrived, and commotion had ensued. Cowhands and vaqueros ran across the open area fetching rifles from the bunkhouse. The four behind him lagged at under two hundred yards. Balum put the roan to a gallop, the men behind him the same, and they charged forward until a rifle shot cracked out over the plain and the riders behind him jerked their horses around and rode back out of range.

# 22

Balum sat at Charles' kitchen table with the Dragoon's cylinder spun open. Angelique sat across from him, the four other chairs occupied by Charles, Will, Tessa, and Juanita. Sara had been seated in a chair, a rope at her waist fastening her to it. Outside, men patrolled the perimeter like soldiers on guard duty. The ranch had morphed into a temporary fortress.

Balum bent over the revolver and measured out a bit of powder which he sifted into each cylinder. He followed each pour with a wad, then a bullet, and compacted them all until they were tight, and swung the cylinder closed.

'It's a hell of a situation,' said Charles, leaning back in his chair. 'What would you say, Will? If you was sitting on a jury. All you know is Balum was on that train along with them bandits and robbed 'em. One passenger dead, shot through the face.'

'It looks bad,' said Will. 'Angelique could testify. She knows why you did it. You didn't have a loaded gun, but who knows that but you?'

'I'm through with the courts,' said Balum. He slipped the Dragoon into the holster on his gunbelt.

'What about her?' Charles motioned to Sara.

Balum kept his eyes on Charles and gave his shoulders a slight shrug.

'You can stay here as long as you like, Balum,' said Charles. 'You and Angelique both.'

'Thanks.'

'But them boys ain't gonna tire. There's no sheriff in Cheyenne. Not since you run off Teddy Boiler. You take the law into your own hands and you'll only dig yourself a deeper hole.'

'I had the law in my own hands. I *was* the law. I had Nelson dead to rights, and no reason to let him live. But I did. All because some Eastern dandies got their knickers worked up about due process and salvation and I don't know what else. And look where it got me. No. I'll deal out the sentences this time around.'

'Even if you battle it out with the four that are left,' said Will, 'even assuming you kill every last one of 'em, this girl needs to be taken to trial. You can't just hang her. Folks won't stand for it.'

'People don't like the idea of hanging a woman,' said Charles.

Will took a look at Sara tied at the chair.

There was a moment of silence, and Angelique spoke up. 'You two know Balum. Just as well as I do. We all know what's coming. There'll be a trip to Denver and several dead men along the way. So let's not waste time moaning about the injustices of the law, and get you prepared for that ride.'

'Is that what you're planning, Balum?' asked Charles.

'Angelique's right. That girl deserves to hang by a rope, but it won't be my hand that ties the noose. She needs to go through the system, as shoddy as that is. As for the others...I gave the courts their chance and they failed. Those men escaped justice once. It won't happen again. If I ride down to Denver with Sara in tow, they'll follow. They won't want me reaching town with her across my saddle. It'd put screws into their whole story.'

'Stay the night at least,' said Will. 'Don't go riding off tired and hungry and without a plan.'

'You're right, Will. Let's get that grub served.'

They ate chiles rellenos and tamales filled with rajas. Everyone's eyes teared and their noses ran from the picante searing their palates, but they continued eating anyway, Juanita's cooking earning no second places. Sara sat watching from the far wall. Her stomach grumbled but she said nothing.

They left her tied there all night. Ropes were secured over her feet, her hands pulled behind the chairback and bound at the wrists, and another coil of braided rope looped over her chest and tied in a double knot at the back.

'You'll never reach Denver,' Sara hissed when the ropes had been checked. 'My father and Uncle Frederick will shoot you down and leave your dead body to rot under the sun.'

Balum looked at the soft lips forming the words. Lips he had kissed. He looked into her eyes, eyes of a woman he had fooled himself into thinking he loved. He had no response for her, and none did he give her.

Night had come. The ranch hands were given instructions to remain awake on shifts. Ten men on, ten men off. They chose areas favorable to making a defensive stand and hunkered down for the night.

Charles had built his ranch house large and spacious, empty bedrooms waiting in hopes of future children, visitors and guests. Will and Tessa took one after determining the danger to be too great to leave the ranch for their own house only a mile away.

Balum and Angelique took another. They closed the door to the comfortably furnished room and immediately took each other in their arms, their lips meeting in the dark, hands running over each other's bodies. Balum threw her to the bed and peeled off his shirt. Angelique shuffled her shoulders out of the straps of her dress and unveiled her voluptuous breasts in the light of the moon coming through the window. She pushed the dress down her hips in one motion, her panties quickly following, and lay on her back with her legs spread apart, her fingers gently playing with her pussy while Balum kicked off his trousers and let his gunbelt fall to the floor.

He mounted her on the bed and she clutched him tightly to her body. Two lovers, their aching for each other unmet for too long. His chest pressed against her heavy breasts, and he clutched them in his hands and bent his head to suck the nipples. She moaned, reached for his swollen cock and pulled it forward between her legs to her soaking pussy. He thrust himself into her, her firm hips wide, eager for him. Their skin pressed together from their cheeks down to their ankles. They breathed in each other's scent, gripped each other's bodies in the frenzy of passion. Their lips met again, tongues running into each other's mouths, tasting each other. Angelique's moans grew louder. Neither cared that others might hear. Their sweat mingled together and their arms wrapped tightly about one another until they orgasmed in unisoned gasps and lay exhausted on their sides still holding on to one another.

The moon arched over the heavens outside the window. Crickets sounded in the distance.

'I missed you, Angelique,' said Balum.

'I missed you too. I'll miss you even more if you let yourself get shot out there on the way to Denver.'

'I won't let that happen.'

'Keep the girl close to you. They won't risk shooting you if she's in the way.'

'I expect not.'

'They'll aim to kill you in the night. It's their chance to get close. Plan for that. Don't waste words in silly talk. Just put bullets into them and haul the corpses into Denver. To hell with Johnny Freed or anyone else's opinion. It's only ours that matters. You do that, and come back to me, Balum. We have a life to start together.'

# 23

A campfire burned a half mile out from the ranch. They'd built it in the mottled ground at the base of a knoll, in the leeward side where the wind wouldn't touch it. By midnight it had whittled down to coals.

The vaqueros watched the flame contract and whither from their selected positions buttressed up along the bunkhouse walls. It spit and cracked and shrank from its flamboyant yellow into orange, and finally a deep and fading red until it disappeared as if the very earth had opened up to swallow it from existence. When it was gone the vaqueros sat and smoked cigarillos and drank coffee throughout the night without incident. When morning broke they could see the men and their horses, watching and waiting from the foot of the knoll.

Balum dressed himself and walked into the morning air. A cow hand pointed out where the men had spent the night. Three men only. Balum counted again. Three men, three horses. He stared hard at the figures in the grass. Shane Carly was gone.

Balum's mind worked over the change. Shane Carly was a weak man, not only in a physical sense, but in his constitution. He had jumped at the chance to ride with big hombres; men he considered top of the chain. But the going had gotten rough. Lead had begun to fly. Whether he'd run off or been discarded out of uselessness, Balum didn't know. Whatever it was, the odds had shifted slightly. They still fell heavily in favor of Aston and Nelson, but it gave Balum a mental strength to see his enemies lose faith.

In the ranch house Juanita had prepared chilaquiles and machaca. The six of them ate in near silence with Sara still tied to the chair where she had spent the night in discomfort. They untied her hands and offered her a glass of water and nothing more. The breakfast was over in the space of a few minutes. It was not a meal of conviviality, though the individuals present found pleasure in each other's company. It was a meal of functionality. A meal filled with silent anxiety, each person's mind on the future.

Charles fidgeted with a mug of atole and finally spun it around and slapped his hand on the table. 'I'm coming with. I can roundup a dozen boys, all loaded down with rifles. Nelson won't touch us.'

'No you're not,' Balum's response was firm. 'This has nothing to do with you. You either, Will. I appreciate the offer and I know it's sincere, but this is a mess of my own making. It's something I'll clean up myself. There'll be a trial. One for Sara, one for anyone else who lives through it, myself included. I need you alive and well to testify as to what's gone on. That's all I ask.'

'If that's the way you want it, Balum.'

'That's the way.'

190

They rose and sent a vaquero to fetch the roan and a spare from the stable. He returned shortly with the animals saddled, fed and watered, and refreshed from the day before.

Sara was the first onto a horse. Her hands had been tied once more and her feet remained bound by the same ropes that had held her through the night. Balum bent and picked her up from the legs and dumped her over the saddle in the same manner as Frederick Nelson had ridden, and no differently than Balum had been thrown over his own horse. Will tossed the trailing rope from her wrists under the horse's belly and Balum winched it around her ankles on the other side. Sara made no sound, no complaint.

'Not a one of 'em has got a rifle, Balum,' said Charles after Balum had swung into the saddle. 'That's an advantage in your favor. So take the Winchester. They come closer than you feel comfortable and you let go a couple rounds. That'll keep 'em a few hundred yards back.'

Balum took the rifle and a sack of cartridges. He laid it across the saddle in front of him.

'Lend me a knife. A big one.'

'I can do that,' said Charles. He entered the house and returned a minute later with a bowie knife sporting a nine inch blade forged from Damascus steel in a leather-bound handle. He held it up to Balum. 'Even Joe would approve of this one.'

Balum took it and looked down at his friends. His eyes held Angelique's the longest.

With his hat, Charles swatted the roan's backside and Balum rode out of the ranch yard with Sara belly-down over the spare horse beside him. He aimed due south and no sooner had he left the premises than the three riders on the hillside took to their mounts and fell in line behind him like a chain of unsmiling pilgrims marching to some drab and sober reckoning.

They made no effort to catch him. Not for the first few miles after leaving the ranch. Balum twisted his head back often, measuring the distance with his eyes, wondering at their intentions. After an hour of riding, the pursuers drew comfort in their judgement that Balum had indeed ridden out alone and his friends had remained behind. They picked up the pace of their horses and began to close in.

Balum turned in the saddle, saw their advancement, and drew his horse around to face them. He raised up the Winchester and set the butt of the stock into his shoulder. At the motion the men scattered like a stone thrown into a flock of birds. Balum sat watching them retreat out of rifle shot, but did not move the roan again for a fair stretch of time. Instead he watched the men sitting their horses out on the plain.

From his saddlebag he drew out a patch of tobacco and pinched a wad with his fingers. He nestled the plug into his cheek and waited a minute, enjoying the warmth of the sun on his arms and legs. After a while he spat.

'Balum,' Sara's voice came from the side of her horse. 'Untie me. Or leave me tied but at least let me sit up.'

'Blood all rushing to your face, is it?'

'It's horrible.'

'Believe me, I know.'

Mucus had gathered at her nose. She coughed and hacked phlegm to the ground.

'I was wondering,' he spat and wiped his face with the back of his hand. 'That ten thousand you stole. Now where might I find that money?'

She breathed heavily but no answer came.

'You let your mind work that over,' he said and turned the roan back south.

They rode at a steady pace, though not a taxing one. The three riders trailing them declined to advance. They rode upright in their saddles with Balum forever in their sight. He sought not to break away, for there was nowhere to hide. The plains stretched open and offered no hiding save for small stands of gnarled pines and cottonwood trees crowded in tight bunches. Occasional dips in the terrain and the rise and fall of gentle hills would afford no sanctuary. Concealment was illusory. Neither was there any need for it. Night would come, and in the cover of darkness a settling of grievances would be metered out in death.

In the heat of the afternoon they stopped at a meandering stream measuring only a few feet wide running between two shapeless swaths of earth that held nothing but woody grass browned from thirst. Shrubby potentilla clutched to the muck at the stream's edge. The horses dunked their muzzles into the water and lifted them dripping and wet when they'd drunk their fill.

Balum drank his canteen empty and refilled it in the

running water. He brought it to Sara and tilted her head to the side with his hand on her jaw and poured some into her mouth. It splashed over her face, some of it running up her nose, and she coughed and spat and cursed him.

'You figure on telling me about that money?' he asked.

'Go to hell. They'll kill you tonight. You realize that? You can't make it to Denver before nightfall, and they'll find you in the dark. You're a deadman.'

'So tell a dying man where his money all went.'

'That's what this is about? I tell you and you'll set me free?'

'No. I won't do that. I'll go light when I testify against you though. Maybe you'll just get a few years in prison as opposed to the gallows.'

'Women don't get hung out here. Not in the West.'

Balum recalled Deborah DeLace. The image of her body swinging from a rope alongside her father, the town of Bette's Creek gathered in silent testimony. Sara reminded him of the woman more than he had first realized.

'Only the worst of them,' he said.

'Not me. You'll be dead by morning. You'll never see that money again. It's gone anyway. Wired out to Kansas City. And all of it legal. All it took was one good cock sucking.'

'They say a fool and his money are soon parted,' rambled Balum, his eyes staring off to the north where the three riders sat. 'At least I had a good time losing it.'

She gave no response other than a snort that sent a

stream of snot to the ground.

Balum mounted the roan again and took up the reins of Sara's horse. They left the stream behind them and rode out under a cloudless sky with the foothills of the Rockies far to the west. The horses flushed out quail and pheasant from the grass, and an occasional rabbit would dart in zigzagged patterns before stopping to look back at the two travelers riding in silence.

Evening approached. The sun turned the flat clouds along the horizon into an array of peach and violet, a glistening ring of gold tracing the outline along each mass of solid vapor. In the east the broken edge of the moon had risen to begin its trek across the nighttime firmament. Shapes lost their sharpness. A grey-lavender hue overtook the land. Riding mercilessly behind them the three figures turned dark.

Balum's eyes had been searching. His mind had enjoyed the full length of a day to consider the coming night. In the darkening window of the evening he reined in the horses on the flat of a long plateau. A few miles to the southeast, a grove of trees larger than most of the frail and thin stands they had ridden past during daylight covered a thick swath of land. Oak and cedar and pine mixed together; enough to form a canopy that stretched over a hundred yards and nearly as wide.

As they waited for nightfall he untied the bandana around his neck. He swung to the ground and fished Sara's kerchief from her dress pocket, then wadded it up and shoved it in her mouth, suffering more than one bite to his fingers as he did so. He wrapped his bandana tight overtop and secured it with a knot behind her head. His fingers quickly worked the rope holding her wrists and ankles together, and when she was free she remained where she was, face-down over the saddle, too weak to move. He coiled the rope and looped it over his saddle horn then mounted up again and raised the Winchester in warning to the anxious men watching from the northern horizon.

The bright oranges and yellows left the clouds. They turned purple, then grey, and the stars above them began to appear out of the night. The three figures in the distance moved, blurred, and when they vanished behind the veil of darkness Balum grabbed up the reins of both horses and charged across the plateau to the stand of black forest beyond.

# 24

In a gallop they crashed into the underbrush of the forest. Branches popped underfoot as they were crushed and snapped by the weight of the horses barreling forward. At his side Sara screamed silently into the gag tied over her mouth. Balum put an arm up to shield his face from the boughs whipping into him, and bent low across the roan's neck as it skittered between trees with the second horse following blindly behind it.

No light penetrated the woods. The sun was gone and the moonlight reflecting from the shaved orb of the moon had not the strength to illuminate what transpired beneath the canopy. He let the horse pick its way along, and in a random spot on the western edge of the woods he stopped suddenly and dismounted. He unlooped the rope from the horn and walked to the horse behind his own.

Sara kicked at him ineffectually when he pulled her from the saddle. He hauled her over his shoulder several feet into the woods until he ran up against an oak with a flat trunk, then spilled her from his shoulder and set her with her back against the bark. The rope he wrapped three times over her arms and chest, around the back of the tree, coiled tight enough to pin her thoroughly, and tied it off in a double knot.

Rising, he paused and listened. The sounds of pursuit had reached the edge of the treeline. He grabbed the reins of the horses and walked gingerly with one arm out until he had left the trees behind him and the pinpoints of starlight opened up above. In the open grass he stopped the horses. For a moment he debated tying them to a tree, but he discarded the idea. If any of the men were to find the horses they would kill them. He had no doubt of that.

Keeping only the rifle, he smacked the two horses across the hindquarters with his open hand and they trotted off into the night. Should he live to see morning he would track them down again.

Into the trees again he turned. The sounds of his enemies had dissipated. Beyond the rustling of the night there was nothing. Crickets chirped, the swoop of a bat overhead. Lightning bugs flickered on and off.

Balum remained motionless until the sounds disappeared into the background of his mind, then bent over and removed his boots. He laid them beside a tree and leaned the Winchester alongside them. From his belt he unsheathed the bowie and judged the weight of it in his hand; how it balanced, how the shape of the blade carved the empty air in front of him.

In silence he sunk deeper into the woods. The pupils of his eyes dilated until they reached the edges of the irises, grasping at light that wasn't there. With his free hand extended before him he took careful steps over the ground, his feet covered in socks only, feeling each branch, each leaf and cone underneath. His movements created no sound that rose above the din of crickets and owls, or the soft buzz of the wind cutting through tree branches.

He stopped often to listen. Like a nighttime creature, blind and navigating by sound alone. At the first hint of sound foreign to that of the woods he froze. He waited and it came again. A man walking. Slowly.

Balum crouched and let his eyes relax. An image of his surroundings formed in his head through the information gathered by his ears. The man on foot was alone. They had separated. The lone man walked slowly, carefully, yet clearly was no woodsman. The soft compression of leaves trampled under boots, an occasional twig snapped, it all gave away not only his position but his trajectory.

Balum rose from his crouch and put a foot forward. Another, one more, and he stopped again. He redirected his path then continued. Seventy or eighty feet he judged to be the distance. More steps. His toes reached out to test the ground before placing the full weight of his body down. His socks had become damp, his feet cold within them. He stopped again and waited. The man, whoever it was, would reach him soon.

Cold seconds went by. The wind stopped. Balum could hear the man's trouser legs chafing against one another.

When the man's breath became audible Balum rose from his crouch. The man stopped. His breath caught.

'Aston?' the man whispered. 'That you?'

Douglas Crenshaw. Even in a whisper Balum recognized the voice of the fat lawyer. A quick succession of four clicks from a Colt hammer being cocked back advertised the presence of Crenshaw's weapon, and Balum came forward bent low, the bowie ready in his right hand. His left hand groped out and found Crenshaw's shoulder. The shoulder flinched, swung down, and Balum thrust his right arm forward and sent all nine inches of the blade through the lawyer's belly.

The Colt blasted from Crenshaw's spasmed finger and a flash of light lit the image of the two men locked in some horrid embrace of death, a slice of a second only, before darkness swallowed them again. Balum's left hand pushed Crenshaw's gun hand away and in the same motion he drew the knife out from the man's belly with the squishing sound of tripe being sliced, and plunged it in again.

Crenshaw gasped and let out a moan a beast might make as it lay dying. His fat body fell backwards and Balum stabbed the bowie through the massive torso several times over, the wounds squirting like demonic geysers spewing spindrift of hot gore onto Balum's face.

Somewhere to Balum's left, two gunshots clapped through the woods from a distance of under fifty yards. Balum lunged forward over Crenshaw's body, feeling for the head, and when he found it he brought the blade to the man's neck and drew it across the length of it, feeling thick blood course down the bowie handle and run over his knuckles.

He jumped up from the dead man's body and ran ten feet with his arms out and stopped. He wiped the blade across his pants and squatted with a tree between himself and the source of the two gunshots.

The night had returned to silence. Crickets started up again while Balum fought for his breath to return to normal. He waited and listened. Whoever had fired those shots was too close to move without making sound. Not that it couldn't be done. But neither Frederick Nelson nor Aston Sanderson were men who knew how to move silently over a forest floor.

A section of time went by that Balum found hard to judge. He could not see the stars nor the moon. Blackness surrounded him and nothing changed. It might have been an hour, maybe four. He had no idea. He waited longer and let his mind work.

Two men were left. If they both remained alive by sunrise, Balum's chances would turn as dark as his present surroundings. The man who had fired those shots lay close by, afraid to move. Balum waited another stretch of time, his feet freezing. He cupped his toes in his hands to warm them. He had no choice. He had to move.

He stepped out from the trunk of the tree and took small careful steps to the source of the gunshots. Every few feet he paused to listen. Nothing but the night. He covered ten feet, then another ten. He stopped. When he stepped out again his heel came down on a small twig of pine and it snapped crisply in two.

A gun roared. The bullet smacked into a tree to

Balum's right and sent bark flying into his face. He sprawled to the ground and rolled, then came up and took four large strides while the echo of the gun rang through the air. The Manhattan Navy; Aston's gun.

The man was not far. Thirty feet, no more. Balum sank slowly to his hands and feet. Like an animal he crawled over the distance, a human spider moving its legs one at a time, ever so slowly. He cut the gap in half and leaned back on his heels.

Aston's position was close but still undetermined. Balum ran his hand slowly along the floor. His fingers brushed over leaves and pine needles until it found the sharp bristles of a pine cone. He picked it up and tossed it underhand into the darkness.

It smacked lightly against a tree and Aston's Manhattan Navy flashed with an accompanying smack of sound, of which Balum took full advantage. He ran with his left hand outstretched and the bowie low in his right. The flash of light had been clear; no trees or branches grew in the remaining fifteen feet. Before he expected it his body crashed into Aston Sanderson. They fell to the ground, Balum on top, but Aston moved fast. He rolled Balum over with a push of his hand and drew back the hammer, its faint clicks clacking in the night.

Balum slashed upward with the blade and felt it catch. Aston fired wildly, the shot unaimed. The bullet pounded into the soft earth beside Balum's head, and Balum ripped the knife through the air again, then rolled, Aston's body beside his, and leapt forward again and caught the big man's neck with his free arm.

Aston dropped backward. The weight of his body crushed Balum underneath. The wind collapsed out of Balum's chest. With his right arm he brought the blade around and stabbed into Aston's ribs. The man seized up, his body lurched. Balum held fast to the neck, squeezing the inner side of his elbow into the thick throat.

Aston's gun barked out again. He had crooked his arm back and fired back over his head, and the blast next to their ears deafened the two of them. Balum brought the knife around again, stabbing into the side and belly of the man on top of him, feeling his own chest being crushed by the weight above him. He drove the knife in again, a sucking sound like boots pulling out of mucky soil, and Aston lurched wildly above him.

The man rolled over and Balum kept his hold over the neck. His right arm found more range and he drove the blade around Aston's chest and stabbed the tip through the ribs and into the lungs. A gush of blood came pouring out of Aston's mouth, spilling down his chin and over Balum's arm at the neck. Furiously Balum stabbed the bowie knife into Aston's chest until the body lay dead and lifeless and the ground around them a puddle of mud, thickened by Aston Sanderson's blood.

Balum crawled through it on hands and knees. Bloodied soil seeped into his trousers, through his socks and along his forearms. He clenched his teeth and struggled to calm his ragged breath until he could hear it no longer. The stench of death clung to him. The blood smeared over his skin and clothing began to dry and turn crusty. It caked along his knuckles and cracked when he bent them. With no thought in his head he waited. He listened. The breeze returned and lightly ran over his face. More time passed and he stood and took steps on feet stiffened by the cold.

Light showed itself on the edge of the woodline. Morning was near. The sun had not yet risen. A burnt-orange aura preceded its apparition from behind the horizon. It came slowly, then suddenly, light cutting through the treetops and disseminating through the leaves down to the dew-covered floor.

Balum's senses turned from sound to sight. His eyes that had been made useless in the fog of night turned sharp and piercing. He rubbed them, shoving back the sleep that lagged behind the lids. Bits of movement caught his attention. A leaf turned in the breeze. Birds darted low through the trees.

As images became sharper he crept to the edge of the treeline and circled closer to where Sara sat with her back against the trunk. The ropes still held her. She sat with her head fallen forward, dozing, her knees curled up to her torso. As he watched her, her head bobbed and she came out of her sleep. Her eyes blinked forcefully and her head turned.

Balum squinted. He saw her eyes dart in search of something. Someone speaking to her.

He leaned forward and walked toward her with the Dragoon having replaced the bowie in his right hand. A movement caught his eye. He swung his head sharply in time to see Frederick Nelson draw his gun and level it across the woods at Balum.

It barked and jumped in the man's hand as Balum hurled his body forward. The bullet whistled past his head and imploded into the limb of a tree. A shower of wood shards sliced the air. Balum turned and fired. Another shot came hurtling across the woods from Nelson's gun.

Through the sound of gunfire a wail rose up from Sara's throat, audible over the gag tucked in her mouth. It came hoarse and cracked, and through its cry Balum fired the Dragoon and saw Nelson's body jerk, his knee buckle, and his frame drop lower.

Balum ran in an arc, tree branches and the trunks of towering pines cutting his view of Nelson into sporadic sections. The big man followed Balum's running figure with the barrel of his gun and fired off shots that sent leaves spiraling downwards where the bullets cut through them.

Balum dropped to a knee suddenly and fired his last two shots into Nelson's body. They hit him, one after the other. They ripped through his chest and exploded in destruction out his back, expunging a ribboned mass of meat and organ out two gaping holes beside his spine. His body leaned back, then fell face forward into the leaves.

Balum plucked the bowie from his belt and ran toward the man. His steps propelled him across the ground, feet cutting sharply on twigs and cones. Descending upon the fallen man, Balum raised the knife.

Like a fabled monster rising from the sea, Nelson's

body rose from the earth. His ashen face bore a grimace made hard by hatred, and he raised his gun hand and fired point blank at Balum. The distance was not more than four feet. Balum had lifted the bowie above his head and the bullet tore through the underarm of his jacket.

The knife came down like a fallen ax. Its tip bit into the bridge of Nelson's nose and the nine inches of blade followed until that same tip protruded out the back of the man's skull.

Frederick Nelson fell back dead with the handle of the bowie sticking out of his face like a long brown nose pointing toward the heavens. In a single jerk Balum ripped it from the man's cranium and turned and crossed the distance to where Sara sat screaming and jerking at the ropes.

Drenched in the blood of his enemies, blood and plasma smeared over his face and clothing, he walked over the cold wet ground like some creature risen from hell and gone mad with fury. Blood and brain dripped from the long blade of the bowie knife. Dirt caked his knees, a dark magenta from the mix of blood and earth. He reached her and stood motionless with the knife a moment. Then he bent and slit the ropes that bound her.

# 25

Movement on the streets of Denver froze in shock and horror as five horses shambled through the center of town. They came out of the setting sun with three of them portaging the dead butchered bodies of blood-drenched men, their straw-like hair blowing askew in the wind. Sara sat her horse with her hands tied at the wrists and her eyes empty and unfocused.

In front of the motley ensemble rode Balum. The blood painted in thick strokes on his face had dried and blackened under the sun. His clothing was stiff with it, caked heavy and dark. It covered his trousers, his hands, the handle of the Colt Dragoon protruding from the holster. He rode with his eyes bored straight ahead and paid no mind to the gawkers and pointers rushing into the street out of the stores and hotels and saloons and brothels.

At the jail he dismounted and hitched the roan to the post out front. He made a motion for Sara to follow, and she obeyed and dropped to the ground. Another motion from his hand signaled her to enter the jail, and when she did he followed her through it.

Ross Buckling bent the newspaper in half to get a look

at the two ghostly souls who had entered the jailhouse. His mouth fell open and the paper sank to the desk.

'Sit down,' Balum said to Sara, and she sat in the chair beside Freed's empty desk.

Ross said nothing. He reclined in his chair and looked at Balum and waited. Balum put a hand to his breast pocket and, finding it empty, felt his trouser pockets until he found the pouch of tobacco. With his blood-blackened fingers he drew out a wad and tucked it into the back of his cheek.

'You got a minute?' he said to Ross.

At no point in the story did Sara interject. She had no arguments, no rebuttals or nuance to add. She hardly seemed to listen at all. When Balum had told all there was to tell he spit a wad of tobacco juice into the spittoon in the corner and turned back to the Sheriff.

Ross Buckling shook his head. 'I don't doubt a word of it. Still, you know what it all means. Another trial. You on the witness stand again, you as the defendant. The robbery happened outside Cheyenne, and seeing as Cheyenne ain't got no law to speak of, it'll mean Freed will be involved. He'll be looking for witnesses. He ain't gonna like this.'

'He doesn't have to like it.'

'You know he was sweet on that girl right there,' he nodded toward Sara. 'He can hardly stand to hear your name spoke without his face pinching all up and his nose flaring.'

'He'll have all the time in the world to sweet talk her then. Until they hang her.' Balum fired another pellet of tobacco into the spittoon and laid his hand against the jailhouse door.

'You're leaving just like that, Balum?' said Ross.

'I am.'

He made to open the door but it opened for him, and Johnny Freed stood in the frame. The Marshal's head jerked back a bit when he saw Balum standing so close to him, and his face scrunched up in anger.

'Are you responsible for those dead men out front?' he shouted.

'You bet I am.'

'Is this your idea of vigilante justice? Revenge? Is that it?' His eyes caught Sara sitting at the chair inside and he pushed past Balum and bent to look at her. 'You poor thing,' he murmured. He swung back around to Balum and took a few sharp steps across the floorboards until he was face to face with him. He rose his hand and stuck a finger out and lifted it to Balum's face where it shook like an alcoholic's digit too long without drink.

'I don't care what your cockeyed story is for this, Balum, I swear to God I will have you hung for these crimes…'

Balum pulled his fist back and drove it into Johnny Freed's face. The knuckles on it were wide and thick and hard from years of labored use. Freed's nose crunched beneath the impact and he fell flat to the floor where his head bounced twice on the wooden boards and came to rest.

Balum leaned down with his hands on his thighs and

209

said to Freed, 'You shut your mouth and do your job. If you need me you'll find me in Cheyenne.' He straightened back up and touched his hat brim with a blood-covered hand and gave a nod to Ross, then left through the door.

He untied the roan and swung into the saddle. The three dead bodies he left hanging over the horses at the jail. He left Main Street and swung down the meandering lane to Chester's cabin. A knock at the door went unanswered. He rode on to the Mexican cantina where the barman with the thick black mustache greeted him and told him he'd seen nothing of Balum's friends.

He found them in the second story of the Silver Nest. Chester and Daniel, immersed in a game of faro. The hall came to a standstill when Balum came in stinking of death and blood and gore and looking like some creature pulled from the swamps of an oil pit fire. His friends raised their heads to see the reason for such silence, and when they saw him they abandoned their game and rushed to him.

It took him no longer than half a minute to tell his story. Details were sparse. He'd told it too many times already. They ordered him a shot of whiskey at the lower level and they drank in somber silence.

'Hell, Balum,' said Chester. 'I'd say you could use a few more of those.'

'One's enough. I've got to be riding.'

'Riding? Where the hell you riding to?'

'Cheyenne.'

'Balum, you need a bath, a good night's sleep, a shave...hell, you need rest. Right here you've got all that, plus me and Daniel here to drink with you. What could be better than that up in Cheyenne?'

Balum set the empty whisky shooter on the bar and looked at his two friends. 'A woman by the name of Angelique,' he said, and a smile grew and stretched across the lines of his blood-streaked face. A smile he had been too long without.

Made in United States
Troutdale, OR
06/26/2023